LOST!

- A themed anthology -

**Presented by
Creative Writing Institute**

**Copyright © 2017
Creative Writing Institute, Inc.
and the individual authors**

All rights reserved, including the right to reproduce this book, or any portions, in any form. The only exception is by a reviewer who may quote short excerpts in a review.

This is a work of fiction. All characters, places and events in this book are products of the authors' imaginations. Any resemblance to persons living or dead is entirely coincidental.

Cover image design © Jianna Higgins

ISBN: 978-1-927296-19-6

Dedication

by Jianna Higgins

We dedicate this anthology to all the writers who suspect they should take a writing course but dismiss it because a) they think they learned to write at school, or b) they have really great ideas for stories and want to get stuck in and write them down.

I was one of those writers. I knew I could write. People told me so. But one day I finally took a course with Creative Writing Institute. Best decision ever!

At first, all the red ink (track changes) bothered me, but as the lessons continued, I realized my writing was changing as I applied what I'd learned. The red ink was less, but I welcomed it because it was all new knowledge.

I learned *I didn't know what I didn't know.* Sounds obvious, but it's so true. I learned better sentence structure, when to use a comma, how to start a story with a bang, what to leave out, character development, world building, plot twists and so much more. My personal tutor nailed me on the rubbish, put smiley faces in the margins whenever she laughed out loud, and she wrote notes that built up my confidence as a writer.

My tutor also taught me Show/Don't Tell, which

helps your reader see the action in his/her mind. Here are some examples from the course *Horror House* where I had to rewrite the first sentence:

1. The mugger attacked his victim. *The mugger grabbed the victim's jacket, and as he reeled her in, he placed his hands around her throat and squeezed until her eyes bulged and no more breath escaped.*
2. The fat guy tasted great. *When I bit into him, he tasted of salt and sweat, and his bright red blood coated my tongue with a warm, coppery flavour.*

As a judge in the CWI contest, I can quickly tell who has taken a writing course and who hasn't. So many stories languish at the tail end of the scoring because the writer executed the greatest premise poorly. Writing style and technique often determine the winner, and these are the main areas where writers fall short if they haven't taken a writing course. Anyone can have a brilliant idea, but presenting it with poor technique can make a potential winner lose.

A paragraph I wrote in one lesson evolved into a multi-award winning series. I know CWI's writing courses helped my stories stand out in competitions.

I encourage every writer to take at least one writing course that offers a personal tutor who is willing to share their knowledge. Take advantage of that opportunity. You won't be sorry.

CONTENTS

Dedication	by Jianna Higgins	5
Foreword	by Cyle Young	11
A Flight in the Night	by Robert B. Robeson	15
Lost and Found	by C.B. Lindgreen	24
The Small Red Dot	by Laura Lee Perkins	32
Love Notes	by Maxine Bulechek	41
Remnants	by Diane Maciejewski	51
The Noids	by Deborah Owen	58
Details	by Jianna Higgins	77
Arpie	by S. Joan Popek	108
Mount Bad Luck	by L. Edward Carroll	124
The Destination	by Emily-Jane Hills Orford	136
The Awakening	by Mikel Wilson	141
Christmas Letter	by Robin Currie	159

The Ambassador	by Caroline Grace	164
Garden of Lost Memory	by Martha Readyoff	175
The Path Home	by Jennifer Doss	189
Saved by the Belle	by Ronnie Dauber	197
Plain Old Regular	by Karen Rush	204
Sea Princess	by Autumn Fenton	218
It's in the Bag	by C.B. Lindgreen	231
Silence	by Kim Kluxen Meredith	236
Food for Thought	by Lauretta L. Kehoe	243
The Expeditioneer	by Lily Medlock	249
Matilijas	by C. Lee McKenzie	256
About Time	by Tomas Marcantonio	264
Nan's Spirit	by J. Lenni Dorner	272
Scattered Debris	by Jaimi-Lynn Smith	282
Early Days	by Caroline Mansour	291
Remember the Sunrise	by Phyllis Campbell	299
The Lucky Ones	by Susan Van Sciver	308

Winter Lilacs	by Cindy Fox	317
Acknowledgements	by Deborah Owen	325
About CWI	by Deborah Owen	327

Foreword

by Cyle Young

Writing is the burden of an artist who can't paint, and the joy of a conscious dreamer. Writing is a way of life, a destination, and a beginning – all tangled up in the throes of creativity. More than anything, writing is an endless journey.

In the winter of 2015, a literary agent at a novelist retreat in North Carolina approached me. The agent asked if I would like to join their literary agency and fill a vacancy left by a retired employee. Four days later, I drove to Pittsburgh, Pennsylvania, to meet with the owners of Hartline Literary Agency. After a brief meeting, I joined the agency.

I became a literary agent, but beyond that, I was completely and utterly lost.

Do you know that there is no school or training for literary agents? There are no courses, books, or independent study programs. There isn't even an apprenticeship system. Essentially, you must figure out how to be a literary agent on your own.

My agency provided a little guidance, but for the most part I was 100% on my own. I had to find my own potential clients, and I had to find a way to convince them to sign with me. In the first month, I learned all about literary contracts, rights, and the submissions process. During that same period, I also signed my first handful of clients.

I felt like I was in the Wild West of the publishing industry. Every other agent was a competitor, even the ones at my own literary agency. When I strolled into my first few writers' conferences, some agents greeted me warmly, but others acted like they held my wanted poster curled up in their fist. I had to learn fast.

Thanks to Google, the Interweb, and Podcasts, I soaked up industry information. My agency's owners helped me connect with publishing houses and editors, and soon enough, I didn't feel so lost.

My confidence as an agent grew along with my editor contact list—now over 400+ editor contacts. When I landed my first major sale, I was hooked. I didn't just want to meander through the publishing wilderness, I wanted to carve my own trail, and that's just what I did.

Now, two years later, I have 100+ clients and a team of 12 junior agents, submission specialists, and interns that have helped me acquire contracts on 80+ books.

This is only the beginning for me, but I share it to encourage you. You don't have to wander through the publishing wilderness alone. You don't have to feel disenfranchised, defeated, or overwhelmed. No two writers walk the same exact path.

You may find a shortcut to success while others take years to relentlessly plod their path.

Like every good adventure, your journey starts one word at a time.

One short story at a time.

One blog post at a time.

One article at a time.

One poem at a time.

One novel at a time.

You can do it!

When you feel lost, frustrated or defeated, force yourself to write. If you have writer's block, make yourself write. If you are sick, make yourself write. No matter what – gain control and make yourself write!

Invest in learning! I exploded on the agenting scene because I didn't give up when I felt lost. I asked questions. I studied. Listened to podcasts. Attended writers' conferences. Soaked up information. Drank instruction. The more I learned, the more opportunities I found to apply my new knowledge. You can do the same.

Immerse yourself in instruction. *Learn your craft*, and you will make more rapid progress.

There is no universal map on how to become a

published author. The only map you need is the one you create. And when you feel a little lost—ask questions and keep on writing!

* * *

BIO: Cyle Young is a renowned literary agent and award-winning author of over 20 writing awards. In just over a year, Cyle sold over 70 of his client's books to publishing houses and currently represents authors who have combined to sell over 20 million books. In November of 2018, Cyle's book, *Live the Dadventure,* releases with Worthy Publishing.

When not writing or representing books, Cyle travels across the U.S. speaking at many conferences, including regional writers' conferences in OH, MI, NC and GA, hosted by his own company, Serious Writer Inc., **http://www.seriouswriter.com**.

Cyle is passionate about training writers through personal instruction and his online writing school, Serious Writer Academy, **http://www.seriouswriteracademy.com**. Learn more about Cyle at his website **http://www.cyleyoung.com**.

A Flight in the Night
by Robert B. Robeson
First Place Winner 2017 Contest

Landing Zone Hawk Hill, South Vietnam, November 15, 1969.

I lay on my bunk listening to waves of monsoon rain pound the sandbagged roof of our underground medical evacuation bunker.

It was located forty yards from the battalion aid station and our helicopter landing pad in Vietnam's northern I Corps, 32 miles south of Da Nang. Water continued trickling down our bunker steps. It had turned the dirt floor into a quagmire of squishy red mud.

We had placed wooden planks from each of our four crewmember bunk beds to the stairs in an effort to keep our leather paratroop boots from becoming even more muddy and waterlogged than they already were.

"What do you think, sir?" my rookie co-pilot fresh from flight school asked. "Will this cruddy weather force the bad guys to keep their heads down so our grunts can rest and regroup?"

"Hasn't stopped them before," I said. "Even if Charlie isn't out there setting ambushes, we still have to deal with his mines, booby traps and bamboo punji stake holes he's strewn around the countryside. They create more casualties than most of the major battles."

"Does the weather ever get so bad that you have to turn down a mission?"

"I've been here ten months and it hasn't happened yet," I said. "You'll learn a lot about flying from our aircraft commanders that you weren't taught in flight school, and you'll learn a lot more about yourself. When people are wounded and dying and it's your job to evacuate them out of their hell holes, you learn to take risks and accomplish things most people wouldn't think possible." I sat with my legs dangling over the edge of my bunk. "The main thing to remember is that we're a security blanket for all the wounded troops, allies and Vietnamese civilians. They depend on us, and we can't let 'em down."

Dust Off was the U.S. Army medical evacuation helicopter's international call sign. Most thought the name originated from the dust our aircraft stirred when we landed in dry areas, but it was actually an acronym that stood for Dedicated, Unhesitating Service To Our Fighting Forces.

At that moment, the aid station's night radio-telephone operator, Specialist Four Billy Bob Trafton, an Alabama native, jerked open our bunker door. His jungle fatigues and field jacket were drenched from a short run through the tumultuous downpour.

"Captain Driscoll, y'all jus' got an urgent mission for two Americans wounded east of Hiep Duc on the side of a mountain," he said in his Southern drawl. He handed me a soggy white mission sheet with the infantry unit's eight-digit ground coordinate, radio frequency and other essential information we needed.

"Why can't everybody just hunker down during a monsoon and leave each other alone for a while?" I groused.

"Sorry, sir," Billy Bob said over his shoulder on his way up the stairs. "I'll be flight-following with y'all until you're back, like always."

"Okay, guys," I said, using a bit of Dust Off dark humor, "let's mount up and go get ourselves shot at."

Billy Bob was a 22-year-old conscientious objector. From what he'd previously shared with me, the reason he was drafted into the Army and sent to a war zone, after he'd adamantly informed his draft board that his religious beliefs didn't allow him to harm fellow humans, was difficult to fathom. Maybe his propensity for talking was the real reason the Army made him a radio-telephone operator and assigned him to a combat medical facility. The military often crammed square pegs into round holes. But Billy Bob loved our flight crews with a passion.

He'd do anything for us, from having food waiting on our landing pad when continuous missions kept us in the air to arranging helicopter gunship cover in critical situations.

After having my unarmed birds shot up numerous times by enemy fire, I'd discovered in my trek from rookie "peter pilot" to aircraft commander that every mission was another opportunity to die. Dust Off flying continually challenged our grit.

Not wanting to make my co-pilot any more anxious than he already was, I didn't explain beforehand the dangers of a night flight in a full-fledged monsoon, in the heart of enemy territory, in mountainous jungle terrain. These facts, alone, had the potential to spike any pilot's adrenaline, and I wanted him to think this was merely business as usual for a Dust Off crew. Though some might believe such a mission was an impossible undertaking, it wouldn't be if we pulled it off.

Seat-of-the-pants, dead-reckoning flying in an inky sky over the jungle can be scary. This was dead-on true when you knew the enemy was somewhere below in the blackness. Unseen, but there. Waiting.

During such moments, I always recalled what my first aircraft commander said. "It ain't the air that can kill you. It's coming back to earth too hard. The rules of gravity in a UH-1H helicopter always apply.

What goes up must come down, and we don't want the *down* part to mean turning us into a Huey sandwich in a rice paddy or a metal lawn dart somewhere in the jungle." Wise words I had not forgotten.

Due to the monsoon and a lack of aircraft traffic, the Hawk Hill Tower was closed. I knew nobody else was crazy enough to fly in that weather, so I made a departure radio call in the clear and climbed to 1,500 feet while being pummeled by an intense aerial waterfall. Rice paddies below had wisps of ground fog swirling around them like disembodied ghosts.

The infantry unit's position became a critical point of reference on my 1:100,000 tactical map, once I'd plotted it before takeoff.

"Looks like the mountains we're headed for top out at 3,500 feet," my co-pilot said over the intercom. "If we lose visual, it could get hairy in a hurry."

"Yeah, but our guys are located on the side of a mountain in a valley I've flown into many times before," I said. "If we can locate them by way of a strobe light or flare, we can always climb to five angels to clear any terrain on our way back to Hawk Hill."

Twelve minutes later, I picked up lights from a Vietnamese village at the base of the mountain range located near the valley.

"Okay," I said to my co-pilot, "turn off our anti-collision and running lights so Charlie won't see us coming low and slow into his neighborhood."

"Roger, lights off."

I notified Billy Bob that we were switching to the FM tactical frequency so he could also change and follow us. Then I made contact with the ground unit and requested a strobe or flare to locate their position. I knew it might be necessary to use our searchlight longer than desired to keep them from becoming a permanent relic on this mountainside.

Their radio operator briefed me on the patients' conditions and emphasized there'd been no enemy contact for thirty minutes. That's when I picked up their strobe light flashes beneath us and hovered down to a landing using my searchlight to break the gloom. We loaded the patients quickly and I pulled in maximum power to begin a climb to 5,000 feet on our way out of the valley.

At 4,000 feet, tremendous gusts of wind buffeted the aircraft and a resurging torrent of rain slammed against our windscreen. I had my co-pilot turn on all of our lights again, in addition to switching our windshield wipers to high, but frontal vision was totally obscured.

"I'm going on instruments, so keep an eye out your side window for any openings below," I told my co-pilot. "Turn the off lights again. They're giving me vertigo in these clouds."

"Right, sir."

At 5,000 feet, violent updrafts and downdrafts tossed our bird up 500 feet and slammed us down again. Pulling in or decreasing power didn't seem to make a difference. We were at the mercy of the elements. The turbulence was so bad, at times, that we were bouncing around the sky like a ping pong ball and I could barely read my instruments.

I had my co-pilot change the FM radio back to our Dust Off frequency, intent on making contact with the aid station and Billy Bob again. Our helicopter was aloft and alone in a sea of clouds, fog and rain. It was then that an unsettling thought emerged. *I am completely and utterly lost*. The worst thing I could do was admit it to my crew.

I recalled an old aviation axiom. "A pilot is *never* lost. He's just temporarily disoriented." Whoever authored that had probably never flown in a monsoon.

Our FM radio had a control switch that could be turned to "home." When that happened, a needle in the course indicator displayed the direction to the station you were communicating with. When the needle was centered, our course would be in a direct line to that station. Since I knew Billy Bob loved to talk, especially alone at night monitoring his radios, if I could maintain a conversation, his transmissions would lead us home and nobody would be the wiser.

"Charger Dust Off, this is Dust Off 605. You copy?"

"Got y'all loud and clear, 605."

During that sentence, I was able to complete a 20-degree turn to the left.

"We're inbound with two U.S. requiring litters and about fifteen mikes out. What's your current weather situation?"

"Understand two litters and fifteen minutes. Still heavy rain and overcast."

I got in another 20-degree turn to the left and my needle centered.

"Request that you turn up the pad lights as bright as they'll go. We're descending out of 5,000 to 1,000 now that we're out of the mountains, so it'll be easier to spot your lights."

"Good copy, 605."

We kept bantering back and forth until I could finally make out faint pad lights through my chin bubble. I continued descending to 500 feet above the rice paddies surrounding the base. Billy Bob had kept us on course without even knowing it.

After unloading our two patients, refueling and shutting down the aircraft, I walked into the aid station.

Billy Bob was in the rustic radio shack beside the dispensary, both feet propped on a desk where his radios were situated. "Y'all made pretty good time in this lousy weather," he said.

"It was really nasty at the pickup site, but we always manage to find our way home."

"Yes, sir, especially when you kept us talking fifteen minutes so y'all could home in on me. Nice job. A while back, another pilot explained to me how your FM homer works. I knew nobody wanted to talk to me that long in the middle of a monsoon at night unless there was confusion in the cockpit."

When anxiety and uncertainty fasten onto a Dust Off pilot like leeches on an exposed artery, it was always comforting to have someone like Billy Bob Trafton from Alabama in the background helping to lead you home, even when he knew our little trick.

Everyone made it back alive, and that's all that mattered.

* * *

Lost and Found
by Constance Lindgreen
Second Place Winner 2017 Contest

He is a very busy man, my father. Right now, he's ranging over the blue hills of southern Ohio, his long legs carrying him to the field where black and white cows are crowding together at the gate, waiting for him to open it so they can amble into the final pasture.

Dad's hair is dark brown and thick. After farming the whole month of July, he's tanned all the way to the tip of his sharp nose. He's wearing his favorite red and black checked flannel shirt today and a rolled-up pair of Uncle Jack's overalls. Uncle Jack never wears anything else, except for Sunday church, Dad says, nodding his head.

The cows jostle and push him, and he pushes back, feeling their heavy flesh, smelling their sweet breath and hot skin, one hand lifting the latch to the gate, while the other guides the muddy haunch of a Holstein. It's noon and he's looking forward to a glass of iced tea and some of Aunt May's blackberry pie.

He tells me stories as I clear our lunch plates. I guess he used to tell Mother the same stories.

Did he tell her about kissing his cousin when she came to visit? I doubt it, but they were married 45 years, so... maybe.

I help him into the living room. I'll wash those trousers tonight. He'd be horrified if he could see the stain where he dropped that bit of egg at breakfast. He's so fastidious. Silver hair always brushed. Shoes always polished. His sinewy arms tremble slightly as he eases into his recliner. He said he hoped he'd die in his sleep or in his La-Z-Boy. I guess that's the way I'd want it, too.

I walk to the kitchen and bring our cups of coffee. He likes his black and hot. I drink mine just the way I did when I was a little kid - milk and sugar, and lukewarm. Dad said they give it to kids that way, over in Europe. I always meant to ask him about that. I remember he said the babies in Germany drank beer. Mom said it was because they ran out of milk, there at the end of the war. Dad doesn't talk much about that time. Mom said he used to have nightmares about the time he was wounded, even though they had a red cross on the jeep. The other ambulance driver died. It was tough on Dad.

I think he's seventeen in today's story, so that would make the year about 1940. He said he lied to the recruiter, enlisted in the Army medical corps and then went to Germany.

Whoops. He's on another track now. I wasn't paying attention. We've left Ohio. I can tell that.

"I was alone, and it was dark. You know how dark it can get in the country? When all you can see is the tiny lights from the stars? That's where it happened. I was in the woods. Holstein…" His eyes are closed as he speaks.

He was in the woods with a Holstein? I'm trying to picture him on another farm. Here in Indiana?

"She was stalking me," he goes on. "And at first I didn't know who it was. Too young to be so alone. Wasn't supposed to be there. Never ever thought I'd have to use my chocolate." He sighs and leans back, pulling the recliner's lever to raise the footrest.

I am completely and utterly lost. A story about cows? It must be a dream he had and he's trying to tell me about it. Or could it be Alzheimers? I don't know how to respond, so I just nod. His eyes are half-closed now. I guess I'll finish my coffee and then do some ironing.

"Wait!" He says, coming to life, his legs still extended. "Where was I?"

"Well, you mentioned a Holstein, so it must have been somewhere on a farm."

"Bring me the Atlas," he says, "and a chair. You're gonna need one."

"We don't have an Atlas anymore, Dad, but I can find something for you on the internet." He doesn't like the computer. At age 89, I guess that's normal. "Should I search Holstein?"

"Not Hol-steen," he corrects. "The proper way to pronounce it is like, 'I drank a whole-stein of beer.'"

I enter Holstein on the search bar. Hmm.

"It says Holstein is a region in northern Germany, near the Danish border."

"That's right. Holstein is where I was shot. Near a little town outside Luneberg Heath. April 10, 1945, it was. We got cut off and driven north, so we were racing to join the Brits."

I probably look blank as I type Luneberg Heath in. Turns out to be where the northern part of the German army surrendered to Montgomery. But that was in May. Once again, I'm baffled. My father's got a funny look on his face.

"Dad, are you trying to tell me about something that happened in the woods in Hol-stein? Are you saying I have a brother or sister in Germany? Because if you are, I'm definitely sitting down."

"Yes and no," he says. "You're right--there could have been someone for you to go and find, but there isn't."

I'm relieved and I guess it shows.

He reaches over and squeezes my hand. "It was Matt's idea to try to get in on the glory. We had already lost contact with our unit. The radio conked out on us, but the last we'd heard was that Monty was on his way up to Jutland, so we headed in that direction. Almost caught up with him, too.

"It was almost night when Matt broke cover. A sniper got him. Killed him outright.

"I got hit by the ricochet. They must not have seen me. I managed to get to a little thicket, cleaned up and waded downstream until I thought it would be safe to get out in the heath."

"Sounds like it would be pretty open and exposed," I said.

"There was a lot of sand and heather, but also lots of trees. There used to be shepherds there. I found a little shelter. All I had was some water, a tin of Spam, and some chocolate. I didn't know if I'd have to get by on those for a while, so I just drank some water. I was in shock, I guess, but I didn't know it. Fell asleep for an hour or so, woke up and it was pitch black. Not a sound, just the stars, but they were mostly hidden by clouds. I've never felt so alone. All of a sudden, I could feel that there was someone else near me, and that they were coming closer. I started crawling away. And then I got shot again – right in the butt – by a slingshot! It was a big rock and it stung so I forgot myself and shouted. I saw someone running away, but with my adrenalin pumping like it was, I caught up with her right away."

"The woman who might have been the mother of a possible sibling?" I feel sort of giddy. Thank heaven there's no half-sister. At least none he knows of.

"Nope. I'm no cradle-robber. Oh, I caught Dorte all right. She was only ten. Thought she was going to be a great huntress and shoot a deer, but all she got was me. She took me home. I admit I bribed her with chocolate. We took her secret route, came in via the barn and – well, from there on, you can probably guess. Her mother, Greta, was alone. Husband gone. Needed help with the farm, and there was a cow that needed milking. We were both lonely, so… well, you can imagine. I was careful, though. Maybe that's what made her so mad. I think maybe she was hoping I'd take her back home with me. Maybe I should have. Used to say that to your Mom when she was in one of her ornery moods."

So, Mom knew, and she didn't tell me! Now I'm peeved. This is a good story. She should have filled me in. "So then?"

"It was a crazy time. I was only there five weeks. I got to the Brits who were happy to have an extra medic on hand until they shipped me back to my unit. When I went back to Germany in '48, Greta was still there."

"Greta? But when I was little… wasn't that the

name of my favorite cow?"

"You bet it was! See, when I got back there the second time, the little witch set me up. She was plenty surprised and told me how happy she was to see me again. She gave me a big kiss. I liked that, I can tell you. Just the kind of welcome I had dreamed about. She invited me to come for supper that evening, and that Ulrik liked to eat at six, so would I please be prompt. Gave me a big grin and then closed the door in my face. Boy, did she put me in my place!"

"So, you had dinner with them?"

"Are you kidding? I drove to Bruges that afternoon, spent the night and went on to Calais. After a week in Normandy, I took the boat to England and came home from there. When I got back I was still pretty irritated, so I named my biggest Holstein Greta."

"Dad!"

"Maybe it wasn't very nice, but that's what I did. Greta, the cow, was fat and stubborn. Good milker, though. Anyway, 'bout two weeks later I went to a church supper. Your mom saw me sitting in a corner. I was feeling kinda lost and she brought me a slice of peach pie, sat down, and asked me about myself. I took that as a sign. Felt like I'd gone from lost to found in five minutes. I asked her if she'd like to go to the movie sometime."

"And then what happened?"

"She said yes she would. We went every Saturday for a month, got married six months later, and you were born nine months after that." He smirks. "Time for my nap," he says, closing his eyes, "now that I've brought you up-to-date on the history of Holstein."

* * *

The Small Red Dot
by Laura Lee Perkins
Third Place Winner 2017 Contest

The fire, like an enraged animal, breathed behind me as I ran through the forest. My neck felt burned.

Embers flew as trees exploded like small bombs detonating. A living beast, the fire pulled all remaining oxygen out of the air as it raced across the forest floor, devouring everything in its path.

And I was alone. This was between God and me. *Would I survive?*

It's odd how quickly we pray when we're afraid. *Please give my legs the strength to maintain a safe distance and my lungs the ability to breathe.*

The fire was angry, seething--a hungry, living thing ready to devour its prey.

Give me strength and courage. Heart pounding in rhythm with my racing feet, I pushed on. The fire's forward motion seemed to pause, and for a moment, I thought I gained a little distance. Suddenly, it leapt over my head and sparks singed my hair. My blouse stuck to my skin. Was it melting? *I'm in real trouble.* The fire had jumped ahead and burned in front of me. *I've got to change direction — but where should I go?*

I panicked and struggled to regain mental focus.

I am completely and utterly lost.

A voice spoke, "Move over, turn left, away from the direct path of the fire."

Where did that voice come from? I'll never know, but I veered to the left, legs hurling down a granite embankment. *Maybe this rocky surface will allow me a few more seconds of precious time, if I can just stay on my feet.*

Ahead, I saw the lake's surface emerge under the smoke-filled air. Through heavy, yet undamaged tree foliage, I could see water. For some unknown reason, an image of baptism rose up in my mind. Maybe the lake, like baptism, reminded me of an opportunity to be saved. *Am I going to be saved? Is that why I thought of baptism?*

The dry, searing air hurt more with each inhalation. I begged. *Please, please give me decisions that will allow me to survive. Guide my feet and mind.*

On I ran, panting for air. The granite embankment leveled out as I bolted toward the water. My feet welcomed the hard, uncluttered surface after the forest floor of branches, leaves and rocks. I took one more deep breath before releasing my final burst of energy. Although trees hugged the shoreline, there was no visible fire ahead--just thick smoke billowing and swirling, occasionally allowing me a glimpse of my only possible escape--the lake.

My heart thumped hard as I broke through the final stand of trees. The smoke hovered, moving in serpentine patterns, but the air looked safer just above the water. *Maybe I can breathe in that space if I can stay afloat.* I climbed across boulders edging the lake and plunged into the water, hoping it was deep enough to support me. I didn't feel bottom. *Good!* But was it cold! *Maybe there's hope. Maybe I can survive until help arrives.* I decided to swim. To where, I didn't know, but I had to put distance between me and the blaze.

I ducked beneath the water, washing my smoke-filled eyes. When I surfaced, the frightening sounds of the fire seemed further away. I kicked off my shoes and swam further out from shore. *Maybe I should have tied those shoes around my neck? And where did I lose my backpack? If only I had the whistle that was tied to it.*

Realizing I didn't have enough stamina to swim very far, I remained within easy range of the shore, but far enough out to protect me from falling trees.

The fire was everywhere now. Deafening sounds. Screams of fleeing animals and screeching birds melded with crackling fire and exploding trees.

I just made it to the water in the nick of time. In that moment, I did not feel alone. Somehow, I had been guided to the lake. I swam for what felt like hours, but probably only 20-30 minutes in reality. I began to wonder if other hikers were caught unaware.

The fire was 12 miles away when I entered the forest this morning. Weather predictions included dropping temperatures, decreasing winds and possible rain. The forest had been burning for two days on the other side of the canyon, but there had been no warning that it might jump the canyon. *How could it spread this far in just a few hours?*

No planes flew over. No warning sirens sounded. But the smell of smoke had intensified throughout my hike. I simply didn't heed Mother Nature's warning. *Will I drown in the lake or will the lack of oxygen and the heat get me first?* The thoughts kept rising, but I pushed them down. *Stay focused. You've made it this far. There is hope.*

My gut said to bear left and swim slowly, but steadily, and keep the shore in sight. My left foot hit a rock. *How did I get so close to the shore?*

A small peninsula jutted out into the lake, but it was difficult to keep my bearings. Everything in me said to stay in the water, keep moving to the left and don't veer far from shore. I pressed on, resting when I must, feeling my way along the bottom of the lake. Suddenly, the land jutted to the right and I had to follow it.

Tiring, I began to count my swim strokes.

Focus. Counting will help. I swam 10 strokes, then treaded water for a count of 10, then swam 10 more strokes. Eventually, I rounded the narrow tip of land. A narrow peninsula? The air felt a little clearer and the fire's fury felt a little more distant. *Thank God. Please guide me to safety,* I prayed.

Slowly I half-swam, half-crawled around the rocky, jutted land mass. There were no trees. The air appeared slightly less acrid. *Keep moving toward survival.*

Then I saw it. Was it an apparition or was it real? A tiny spot of red, emerging from the smoke hovering over the lake, seemed to be moving slowly toward me. There was no discernible sound above the fire's fury. I rubbed my eyes and blinked. It was still there.

What is it? I tried to shout, but only raspy sounds emerged from my smoke-damaged throat. The small red dot appeared to be resting on the water's surface. *Is it real or is it a mirage?*

Knowing that my distance perception might be skewed, I decided to wait in place. Gradually, the red dot grew larger as it slowly drifted toward me. It was a canoe! For a brief moment, I expected to be rescued. Then disappointment reigned.

The canoe was empty. The only sounds were those of the fire's fury.

Finally, I reached the canoe. *What will I find inside?* It was completely empty except for one small paddle. *One paddle is enough! I'll just paddle on one side and then the other.*

Rounding the canoe, I noticed the *Old Town – 17'* manufacturer's label on the right front bow. *Well, that's certainly a familiar name. Now, can it save my life?*

As I tried to peer across the lake's smoke-filled air, I noticed a very uplifting breeze beginning to stir. *Smoke rises, so I should get in, hunker down and slowly paddle away from the fire.* That seemed to be the most sensible course of action and I could feel the heavy, fiberglass canoe beginning to scrape on the rocks.

Don't take a chance on damaging the hull. I pushed it away from shore as I swung one leg over the side and climbed in, lowering myself onto the canoe's ribs to stay lower where the air might be a bit easier to breathe. Slowly, I picked up the paddle and dipped it into the water. With the first draw, the red canoe began to move. As an experienced canoeist, I turned it out into the lake and began paddling three times on the right and then three times on the left, hoping I was moving in a straight line toward the far shore away from the fire.

Is the sun beginning to set or is it the glow of the

fire I see in the sky? I was unsure, but kept paddling. On and on the boat glided through the smoke, which seemed to be somewhat less dense as I paddled further from the fire's inferno. On the map, Alamoosic Lake appeared to be five to six miles across. I remembered seeing an overnight campsite with lean-to shelters on the hiker's map. Could I find it?

Suddenly, I remembered placing that map in my rear pocket this morning. Would it be legible? Unzipping the pocket, I pulled out the damp, folded map and, squinting in the dusk, could barely discern the lake's perimeter. Then I found the peninsula--the only peninsula on the lake.

I cried with relief. *Stop that! Stay focused. Find your bearings.* Straining to see, I could make out the campground on the map. It appeared to be about one mile north of the peninsula, on the lake's east side. *Looks like less than two miles,* I surmised. Slowly, I paddled on. My concentration peaked as I listened for any sound of other humans.

Suddenly, a flare came out from shore. Someone was sending up a signal!

I paddled toward it as I tried to yell. "Help, please, help!" The air was clearer over here and I heard a muffled sound... a boat motor far away. *I must get to it. I must push on faster before they're gone.*

The canoe moved quickly in response to my

renewed strength. Suddenly, a large aluminum boat appeared in the smoke.

I waved my paddle. "Over here, over here!" The boat motor cut off. "Help! Help!" My voice faded. I heard the motor re-engage as the boat moved toward me. *Thank you, God!*

Two rangers were on board. One grabbed the side of my canoe, saying, "Are you Drusilla? We've been searching for you."

"Yes, I'm Drusilla, and I sure am glad to see you."

In the lean-to, I changed into dry clothes. The rangers put medicine on my burns and gave me water before they put my stretcher in the lifeline helicopter. At the hospital, they said I had second-degree burns, mostly on my arms and neck. My lungs ached from the heat and smoke, and they took a few weeks to recover, but soon I was back to hiking again. The burns left a few small scars--eternal reminders of my gratitude.

No one perished in the Alamoosic Fire, and I learned to be much more careful before venturing out alone into the Maine wilderness.

But that day, I knew I wasn't alone. Some might call it intuition. Some might call it a guardian angel, and still others might say God guided me. Whatever the term, I will forever be grateful for being lead to safety.

    I placed a small, red, circular sticker on my bathroom mirror to remind me how lucky I am. That small red dot probably saved my life.

* * *

Love Notes
by Maxine Bulechek
Honorable Mention Winner 2017 Contest

Lillian Cooper drove her rented car cautiously on the unnamed gravel road, the windows tightly closed and the air-conditioner set to maximum. Iowa in August was unbearably sultry. Her black dress wilted, the linen skirt wrinkled and stuck to her in spite of the recirculating breeze from the vents. She doubted the accuracy of the blinking green arrow on the car's navigation system. Her cell phone showed no bars. She passed another closed gas station, an abandoned oasis in a rolling valley of cropland.

"No place to ask directions. No place to eat. What am I doing here?" Lillian spoke aloud in the humming car, but knew why she ventured out in 70% humidity.

Her mother, comfortably at home in California, urged her to attend a second cousin's funeral in Ashton, Iowa.

Lillian had never met her mother's cousin, but Mother wanted someone from 'our branch of the family' to be there.

To her brother's relief, Lillian volunteered to attend the funeral.

I am lost in the land of Closed on Sunday, Lillian thought. Cresting another hill, Lillian saw the top of a white church steeple in the distance. In the next valley, a sheriff's SUV blocked the road, a bored officer leaning against the emblem on the door, clipboard in hand.

The deputy penned something on his clipboard, then approached and motioned for her to open her window. "License and registration."

Lillian passed him the documents, noting his nametag. "Was I driving too fast, Officer Fajfar?" Lillian asked, confident in her silent 'j' pronunciation in the Norwegian name.

He silently studied her driver's license, compared the picture to her face, then went to his vehicle and climbed into the driver's seat. Ten long minutes later, he returned. "Have you lived in Seattle long?" he asked.

"All my life. My parents are from Iowa. Can you tell me what this is about?" When the officer shook his head, Lillian continued, "I'm here to attend Carol Manning's funeral. She was my mother's cousin. I've been driving on these unnamed roads for over an hour. I am completely and utterly lost. Is this Ashton?"

He nodded, gave her the documents and a dismissive sideways wave. "Have a nice day."

The church steeple beckoned, and Lillian pulled into the parking lot five minutes late. She hurried as much as possible with the heels of her black Jimmy Choo shoes sinking into the gravel with every step. She slipped into a pew in the second row from the back.

Several people turned to look at her and whispered, "Lottery winner" and "Love… life."

Lillian wondered who they were talking about. She glanced at the crowd but saw no familiar faces.

The funeral director reached from the center aisle to hand her a program.

Lillian hid her surprise when she realized she was at the wrong funeral. Conrad Riker? She folded her hands in her lap, crossed her ankles, and straightened her spine. *I'm not leaving early after arriving late,* she thought. *I'll just have to endure it. What will I tell Mother?*

After the minister spoke, people recounted Conrad Riker's contributions to the fire station, a new hospital wing, the handicapped-accessible playground, the stage in the town square, and an annual bonus for all 92 school employees. Many attributed anonymous gifts to Conrad, too. Apparently, this civic-minded lottery winner invested and shared his wealth.

Two hours later, the people in the front row finally stood and filed toward the exit. A woman stopped and stared at Lillian. "Laura! There you are. We knew you would come." The procession line halted, and everyone looked at Lillian. "Well, come on, join us." The woman took Lillian's forearm and compelled her to leave with the nearest kin.

"I'm sorry," Lillian said, when they stopped in a room filled with dining tables. "You have mistaken me for someone else. I'm Lillian Cooper. I got lost and accidently attended the wrong funeral."

The tall, slender woman gathered Lillian in a brief hug. "We know you have to say that. Conrad asked us to delay his funeral to give you a good cover story. We've been waiting weeks for someone else to die. I'm so glad you're here. I'm Silvia Sutton. Conrad was my uncle. Witness protection changed your name to Lillian?"

"No. I really am Lillian Cooper, and I shouldn't be here. I'm sorry for your loss. I didn't mean to intrude. Please excuse me." Lillian found her path blocked by Conrad's relatives. A uniformed police officer stood at the front entrance. A woman wearing a navy suit and an earpiece stood near the back door.

The man standing next to Sylvia spoke in a deep baritone. "He predicted you would say that. Uncle Conrad talked about you so much, we feel we know you. I'm Kent Sutton, Silvia's husband. Look, we'll follow your lead and pretend you are at the wrong funeral. Uncle Conrad was a good man, except for that one mistake, and he spent his life trying to atone for it."

Kent's shiny dome moved slightly as he spoke, distracting Lillian from his words.

"You were the love of his life. He never married. This town became his family. So, even if you aren't Laura, please stay, eat, and let the town be comforted. Sharing their memories of Conrad with you provides closure. It would be your good deed for the year."

"We didn't know about the incident until a few years ago when Uncle had a stroke and started talking about his past. You protected him when you turned state's evidence. He never forgot that you gave him a chance."

"What incident?" Lillian asked. *Though I'm afraid to find out.*

Silvia gently squeezed her arm. "You know we'll never tell."

Lillian looked at Conrad's other relatives who nodded in agreement. She thought about the closed restaurants she had driven past and looked at the loaded buffet table. "Okay," she said, thinking, *I am lost but at least I won't be hungry. What can it hurt?*

She stood with the relatives, allowing the mourners to hug, pat and relate improbable tales until she felt well acquainted with Conrad. Silvia introduced her as "She calls herself Lillian, now."

A few townspeople gave a conspiratorial wink.

Lillian finally eased to the door, but Kent and Silvia stayed with her.

On the church steps, Kent withdrew an envelope from the inside pocket of his charcoal gray suit. "Conrad made me promise I'd give these to you. The last few years he wrote you a love note every day."

"He read a few to me. Some of his poetry is awful, but he wanted you to know he never forgot you," Silvia said.

Lillian shook her head. "I can't accept. You keep them, maybe publish them as part of Conrad's legacy. I'm not Laura." Lillian made it to her car and struggled not to squeal the tires as she left. At the edge of town, she drove past the empty church where she should have attended Carol's funeral. Scaffolding covered one side, bundles of shingles lay stacked under a ladder, repair work obviously in progress. She glanced back and noticed an envelope on the back seat. *Oh No! What am I going to do with sappy love notes?*

She parked at the curb, reached over the seat and grabbed the heavy envelope. She broke the seal and stared at four sparkling stones nestled in hundred-dollar bills.

Suddenly the car rocked as a big woman flung open the passenger door and settled her bulk inside.

Lillian gasped and dropped the envelope. She remembered the woman, the largest nurse in the group from Conrad's nursing home. "I see you have my love notes." The woman lifted the envelope and looked inside. "Not quite what I expected," she mused. "Thought he spent it all on his hometown and lottery tickets. I never suspected Conrad's gift for money laundering." She smiled, and Lillian felt her tension ease slightly. "What are you planning to do with them?"

Lillian said honestly, "Nothing. I just found it in the car. Are you Conrad's Laura?"

"Not for a long time. I've been working part-time at the nursing home to be near him for the last two years. He didn't recognize me. Funny how an extra hundred pounds or so can make a woman invisible." She patted her rounded tummy and continued, "It's mostly padding, but no one looks closely." Lillian noticed delicate wrists and hands, the excess size carried only around the woman's midsection. "Seeing you stand in for me today cracked me up. I always wondered how Conrad's family would treat me."

"Why didn't you introduce yourself? They were really nice."

"It's complicated, but I guess you deserve the truth, and I'd enjoy telling it just this once. After high school I left the Wisconsin farm where I was born for the bright lights of Chicago. I found a job at The Moscow Bar. The owners had Russian ancestors. They decorated the main lounge with huge pictures of Arctic Desert Moss. Intricate-laced green and red lichen or geometric yellowish orange blooms that don't grow in the United States. They decorated the back room with, if you can believe it, pictures of red dairy cows called Tambov, in scenic Russian locations. I'm not sure the customers got the 'moss' and 'cow' joke.

"Anyway, a Russian bakery supplied ethnic pastry and Russian-speaking customers filled the place. I don't speak Russian, but the bus boy insisted one group of regulars were members of the Russian mafia. In the six months I worked there, I learned their names and tried to avoid them.

"Then I got a clerk job at a jewelry store. The manager, Ted, was a total jerk, always trying to paw me and standing way too close. One afternoon three masked men came in with guns held at their sides. One forced Ted into the back room, while the others made me open the safe and place the loose diamonds in a bag. Ted must have pushed the alarm because police swarmed the place, assaulting us with lights and sirens. The robbers disappeared. In the confusion, I put the bag in my pocket.

"When the police interviewed me, I told them about the Russian mob and mentioned every name I could remember from the Moscow bar. No one asked if I had the diamonds and I forgot about them until I got home. They offered witness protection for identifying them and they let me tell my boyfriend, Conrad, goodbye. I passed the diamonds to him and asked him to secretly return them. I was sure no one would believe I forgot about two million in diamonds. Later, I learned the jewelry store filed an insurance claim for *twenty* million dollars. Conrad disappeared. The robbers were never caught, and the Russian mob might be kinda mad at me."

"Kinda?"

The woman shrugged. "Doesn't matter anymore. Money is only good for what it can buy. It can't buy real love, though Conrad gave it his best shot."

They both looked at the brick fire station across the street.

"I left protection, searched for Conrad seventeen years, planning to get married and leave the country. Instead, I heard him reminisce about Laura and watched his efforts to redeem a guilty conscience. I've lived a good, simple life. Wish I never took the diamonds, but I couldn't undo the past. Now I focus on helping others build a future."

Using the roof and door handle for leverage, the woman stepped out of the car. Lillian held the envelope out to her. "I believe this is yours."

"You want them?"

Lillian shook her head vigorously.

"Smart choice." The woman closed the door.

Lillian drove slowly, aware of law enforcement vehicles parked on side streets. At the stop sign, she looked in her rearview mirror and watched Laura stuff the envelope into the church donation box.

* * *

Remnants
by Diane Maciejewski
Honorable Mention Winner 2017 Contest

Clouds the color of bruised plums bear down upon the sunset. Stepping high and slow across the shallow lake, a solitary crane pursues his evening snack. A frog croaks farewell as a blackbird takes flight, revealing a smidgeon of Chinese red beneath its wings.

This place is in my blood. It soothes my soul, and yet, I tremble. I am completely and utterly lost. Lost in the arms of a stranger. I walk here with him of my own accord from the house behind the trees.

"Our home," he says. He'd brought me here from the other place, the noisy place with the rocking grannies and cursing old men. The place of cries and complaints, and moans that unsettle the silence of the night.

"I hate that place," I say. "Don't make me go back."

"No, never again."

After settling me against his chest, he removes two bottles from a brown shopping bag. "Our favorites," he says. "A French Bordeaux for me, a late harvest Riesling for you." He pulls out the Riesling's cork and hands me the half-full bottle. "You must be thirsty from the walk."

There's no glass, so I tip back my head and drink straight from the bottle. Before I swallow, I hold the wine in my mouth, swishing it, savoring the treat. Beneath its sweetness and the suggestion of apples, there is a hint of bitter taste.

As if he's done this many times before, he builds a campfire from kindling stacked nearby. The fire's crackle begs for fluffy, white… something's roasting at the end of a sharpened stick. Hoping he brought some along, I reach for the bag at my feet, but stop when I notice my legs. Bare from the knees down, they are swollen, and blue veins bulge, forming a bumpy boulevard down my calves. I bend my knees to get a better look and wince. They're stiff and painful from walking. I turn my head into the stranger's white beard. "What's wrong with my legs?"

"They've been like that for years."

Years? How is it I've never noticed? "Can they be fixed?"

He shakes his head and his mouth turns downward as though he's sorry to give me the bad news, but his voice is soothing as he talks of the breeze that rearranges the shawl around my shoulders. I like him. He doesn't pinch me with needles or urge me to swallow spoonfuls of applesauce with pills lurking within. He's kindhearted. Gentle.

    Careful not to dislodge his arms, I twist around and study his face. His bottom lip is very full compared to the top, and his nose has a mole near its tip. "Have we met before?" I would like it if we had. "What's your name?"

    "David."

    I know a David, but he's young, with dark hair that skims past his shoulders and lays thick and wavy between my fingers when we neck in the back seat. Father hates his hair. He calls him hippie and stumblebum and threatens to give him a haircut if he keeps me out too late. But the top of this man's head is bald, and what's left of his hair matches his beard. "Are you Santa?" I stifle a yawn.

    He kisses the top of my head. "I'm your husband." Wrapping my hand around the bottle, he urges me to drink.

    "Husband?" Remnants of memories flit across my mind forming a loosely-sewn crazy quilt of our life together. In one square, I sit by his side, rowing across this very lake. In another, I chop vegetables near the kitchen sink as he tosses pasta with grated cheese. In still another, we lie together on a bed, running our hands across one another's bare backs.

    "How long?"

    "We married in '73."

"Was I beautiful?"

"So beautiful that when you walked down the aisle on your father's arm, I forgot how to breathe."

"And now?"

He does not hesitate. "More so than ever."

I sip at the wine and enjoy the idea that I am beautiful until light from the campfire glints off the ring on my finger. "Were we rich?"

"We always had what we needed--and more. I was a physician."

"Was I your patient?"

"Other than your allergies, you were rarely sick. I stitched up your finger once when you cut it slicing a Christmas roast." He takes my hand and traces a thin, white scar. "See?" His lips brush against the inside of my wrist, then linger there until the kiss becomes a prayer.

A name flutters past like fluff from a cottonwood tree. "Who's Carrie?"

"Our daughter."

From across the years, the fresh scent of mowed grass, the smoky aroma of grilling meats, and the tang of barbecue sauce reach my nose. The sun warms the back of my neck. Aunts and uncles and grandparents chatter. Laughing children run between them playing tag. As I set seven candles atop a pink-iced cake, a girl's high-pitched scream cuts through the screech of car tires.

I struggle against the man. Why does he act as if he doesn't hear? I try to pull from his arms, but I'm shaking and surprisingly weak. "Please, let me go! Please. She needs me." He holds me tighter, and tears fill my eyes. Why won't he help? "Do something. Please."

"Shh, shh," he repeats as if I were a colicky baby. "You'll see her soon."

With that promise, my fear oozes, drop by drop, into the roots of the trees around us. When I am calmer, he urges me to drink again.

A twig snaps. An animal like a large dog, but with longer legs and a short, upright tail walks to the lake. It dips its head, drinks, then lifts its muzzle to spear me with its eyes. If I were not so sleepy, my eyelids not so heavy, I would sling my arms around its neck, climb upon its back, and ride across the sky. "What is it?" I ask.

"A deer."

No. No, there is another word, almost the same... reindeer. Yes, reindeer. Dasher or Dancer or Prancer. I was right. This man is Santa, though his chubby cheeks are sunken, his rosy glow is sallow, and the sparkle in his eyes is dimmed. And the season is all wrong, I'm sure of that. Unless I'm at the North Pole... but then there would be snow and ice, and elves pounding and sawing and painting toys for children who have been good all year.

After I take several more sips, fairies dressed in peachy organdy appear. Their magic wands twinkle on and off in the dimming light. I see them swooping and sweeping, twirling until they scuff the magic from their slippers and scurry toward their forest homes. My head swims, and I long to fly off with them. Free. Free of my sweaty palms and racing heart when people demand to know the day of the week, the year, the President's name, and my own.

"How long can I stay here?" I ask.

A shudder passes through Santa. "Long enough to enjoy the moon."

And he's right. The clouds part like stage curtains and showcase the moon, round and fat and sassy. The man who lives upon its airless surface enters from the wings and winks. I hold my breath, waiting for him to speak a magical invocation that will restore me to myself, but he is as silent as the two of us who gaze upon him.

I try to grasp the bottle, but it slips from my hand. Santa holds it to my lips, and I lick the rim to enjoy the last drop.

"Good girl," he says with a catch in his throat.

The sky spins around me, and then I am spinning across the sky. In my bare feet, I pirouette, chassé, and execute an arabesque across a moonbeam until I am out of breath. My eyes close against my will, and I slump against Santa.

He lays me down and rests my head upon his lap, careful of my comfort. Softly, at first, hesitantly, as though he hasn't done it for ages, he sings my favorite song. A song of yesterday when troubles were far away. He brushes my hair from my face, and his eyelashes graze my cheek as he gifts me with hummingbird kisses. "I love you," he whispers.

With that, my heart remembers. I try to say his name, to tell him how much I love him, but my lips refuse to move.

And now, I am the remnants of the quilt. Several pieces fly off to distant stars. One lodges in a craggy crevice of the moon, while another skims across the grass like a crimson leaf on a windy, autumn day. The final scrap seeks out the lake to float upon its still water.

I am completely and utter…

* * *

The Noids
by Deborah Owen
CEO, Creative Writing Institute

"Why do you sing, Mater?" Shazar said. "It is unlike you to make melody."

"Because I am in knowledge of something you do not know," Mater said with a twinkle in her eye.

"Is it about my birthday?"

"Indeed, it is."

Shazar sprang from the floor with jubilance, pinging up and down like a bouncing ball.

"Now put an end to that juvenile foolishness," Mater said. "This is your first day to train as a space jockey. You must be mature and dependable."

"I have waited all my life for this day," Shazar said, eyes aglow. He quit pinging, but his feet continued a happy dance with measured activity.

Mater laughed. "All ten years?"

"Yes. That is a lengthy term at my age."

"I suppose so," she said, hiding a smile.

"When can I pilot the big spaceships? When I am grown, I will be the best Space Passenger Master of all time."

"You may begin Space Passenger Master training in ten more seasons," she said. "You have a while to wait. Enjoy growing up."

Pater's air jet connected to the landing pod outside. He walked in at precisely the proper time and all three took their seats at the table.

"You may ring for the robot, Shazar," Pater said. "And after we dine… " Pater looked at Mater and both grinned, "…we will take you to the pet store to choose a Noid."

"A Noid!" Shazar popped out of his chair and attacked each parent with a loud whoop and squashing hug. They sat motionless, enduring the outburst.

Pater shook his head. "I truly have no idea how he inherited such emotionalism," he said to Mater. "When we received our license for reproduction, we clearly ordered a male with no emotionalism in his DNA."

"I think the android assigned to us had not completed its training. Be tolerant, my mate. He is perfect in every other way. One of the brightest ever conceived, they say."

"I try, but it makes him look, well, you know. Especially in the public eye. If litigation against robots and hospitals had not been outlawed a century ago, I would be tempted to sue them."

Shazar backed away and bowed deep. "I forget myself," he said. "Forgive my outpouring, but it is because I have craved a Noid for many seasons and thus, my exuberance springs without effort."

Shazar bowed to his mother and both parents acknowledged with a short salute. After the dinner hour, the three visited Ammon's Pet Store and Shazar's eyes glimmered with glee. "Look at the Noids!" he said to his parents. "They have the best selection I've ever seen." Shazar ran ahead.

"What are these Noid things?" Mater said. "Where did he see them?"

"They have been advertising them on International Air Waves for twenty-eight days," Pater said. "They were thought to be extinct, but someone found a new supply and imported them. Poor things must be homesick, but they say they make good pets because they are small, are usually obedient, and eat little." They joined Shazar at the Noid Pen.

"So that is what they look like," Pater said as they walked up to the cage. "How very strange."

"*Ugly* is a better word," Mater said, a shiver passing through her.

"Mater, see how they walk upright like us? For the most part, they are just smaller. It must be frightening to be so tiny. I could hold both of them in one hand," Shazar said.

"Yes, but look at the strange appendages on their upper half. They seem to fly about for no particular reason. Maybe we could pinch them off," Mater said.

"That would be cruel, unnecessary and very painful."

"Alright, alright. Leave the frightful appendages as they are," Mater said. "I shall look at something more becoming while I wait."

Pater pointed at a fine looking Noid, and it seemed to stare back at him. "Look at that one, Shazar. It looks like it knows we are talking about it."

"Indeed, it does. I will train my Noid, Pater. I will have the smartest Noid in the kingdom. It will win contests and bring prestige to our lineage."

"Impossible," Mater said, drifting by. "They have no brain, and are therefore untrainable."

Pater raised a bushy eyebrow. "I believe almost anything is trainable, at least to some degree."

Mater frowned, drew near and whispered, "You know it is unlawful to disagree in the presence of the child."

"Yes, and I know how much you like to take advantage of that law," he whispered back.

Her face turned a light shade of blue, indicative of disapproval. "Mind your mouth or I will have the authorities put you in stasis!" she said before she strode away in a huff.

Unmindful of the conversation, Shazar said, "Wait and see, Pater. I will be the best trainer in the new world. I will be patient and kind and my Noid will love me."

"You are falling into emotionalism again, Shazar. Try to refrain."

"I ask forgiveness, Pater, but there is something about emotionalism that makes me feel warm and fuzzy inside. Why do our people not want it?"

Pater stared, caught off guard. "Because I... we... have no need for it. It is impractical."

"But I think..."

"I like that one best," Pater said, changing the subject.

"I was just thinking the same thing," Shazar said, falling into the trap. "I want that one."

"Question. Why do you want such a dreadful looking pet? Does it have any practical use? And which ones are the females?"

"I like Noids because they are unique, and I fail to understand them, so it is a matter of curiosity. As for which are females, I remain unsure," Shazar said.

"Wait here and do not handle the merchandise. I will gain information."

Pater returned with a helper who bobbled along with a peculiar gait. He only had three hands, and Shazar wondered how he could function with such a handicap. Pater leaned over and whispered, "Do not stare."

"Forgive," the child said, looking down.

The jolly three-handed fellow wore a perpetual grin below a pointy nose. "Which did you choose?" he said.

"That one!" Shazar said. "See how it touches me when I reach down to it?"

The smile left Jolly's face, and he shook his head. "Profuse apologies. Profuse apologies. That one is half of a set. I separated them last season and both nearly terminated. They are much too rare to let one die, so the owner traded it in for another. It is a male, and his female is the one standing by the doorway of the hut. If you like the male, you must accept the female as well.
Shall I wrap them up for you?"

"Can they bear more Noids?" Shazar asked.

"I have no records on this set and no knowledge, but most can."

"I want little Noids. Lots and lots," Shazar said.

"We will take them," Pater said, "and we will also take whatever dwelling you recommend for them. Oh, and Noid food."

"Very good. Very good," the chuckling three-handed fellow said.

Shazar spent the evening hovering over his new pets. He fed and watered them, held them on his lap, talked to them and petted them until they grew weary.

Mater entered the room and smiled at her son

and the Noids. "Be gentle. They are delicate little things. And don't let Gordeen near them. They would make a tasty meal for that big lizard."

"Gordeen had not entered my mind. He is sly and would certainly eat them if he could. I obey."

The Noids did not seem to grow over the following season, so Shazar assumed they were adults. Very smart, as well. He greeted them daily in his own language, and they soon learned how to greet him. They also learned other words, like *good night, food, drink, play, Mater and Pater.*

Pater was very pleased at Shazar's training and the pets' progress, insomuch that he and his son played with the Noids nightly.

"Listen, Pater. Did you hear that? I think the male is laughing."

"Do you, now! Would that not be amazing! Why do you think they can laugh?"

"Because they are in a good mood when they make that sound, and they try hard to obey. I have also ascertained that they communicate well with one another in musical tones pleasant to the ear. I am beginning to learn their language, and they are learning ours."

"Noids cannot learn our language," Pater said with a laugh, "but I do believe they are much more intelligent than we think. They can obviously communicate with one another, and they seem to be very trainable. By the way, on another subject, I bought a new pen for the lizard tonight as he is outgrowing the old one."

"For Gordeen? Marvelous! He will enjoy the extra space. I'll put flowering plants and trees in his pen, so he can feel secluded and concealed. When I finish with it, the pen will look like his natural jungle surroundings. I think I'll move the pen to the far corner, under the indoor trees and vegetation. It will feel more like a jungle hideaway."

"Good idea. I must go. Remember to appear at the proper time to dine," Pater said.

"Yes, of course. I will put Gordeen's new pen in the corner and decorate it to his pleasure, and then let the Noids run loose while we dine."

"Run loose?" Pater said.

"Yes. I want to reward them for their excellent behavior."

"An excellent idea. You are a thoughtful master, my son."

Shazar worked on Gordeen's pen and placed the lizard in it. Gordeen sniffed the large water bowl and foliage and disappeared in the bushes at the back of the pen.

Shazar smiled, and turned to the Noids he had named Plume and Ovaplume, or Ova for short. "Come to me, little Noids," he called, and they jumped on his hand. Shazar smiled. "I have a surprise for you. You may play in my room while I eat tonight. I shall return after I dine." He placed them on the floor, but they huddled together in the monumental surrounding. "Go on. Nothing will hurt you. Explore and have fun," Shazar said, nudging them until he accidentally knocked them down. "Plume, Ova, do you understand?"

They nodded.

"I do not think so, but maybe someday." He sighed. "I am rewarding your excellent behavior. Play and have fun. Do not fear. If you get lost, I promise to find you." And with that, Shazar vacated the room and closed the door.

Ova and Plume hesitantly explored cracks and holes in the floor. Their two tiny legs carried them to the jungle in the corner and Ova took great delight in climbing the vines that hung from the tree. Musical tones erupted in a steady stream as they spoke, and if one had an interpreter, their conversation would have sounded something like this:

"I'm going to climb the tree vines," she said. "Come with me, Plume."

"I got my exercise pulling you out of the hole. You really must be more careful. I'll climb the tree with you and take a nap in the fork while you look around. Call me if you have trouble."

"Nothing can hurt us in here."

"Tell that to the hole that almost swallowed you," Plume said. They climbed together--he on the branches and she on the vines.

"I love Shazar," Ova said. "He's a good master. If we can learn his language and tell him how we came to be here, perhaps he'll take us home."

"That's a lot to hope for, but it's not a bad idea. Let's try harder to learn his language."

"He is brilliant, to be sure, but a teacher he isn't!"

"True," Plume said, "or we would have already mastered his language." Plume sat quietly and in deep thought.

Ova pressed closer and leaned against him.

"I'm sorry," Plume said. "I promised to take care of you. I had no idea slavers would come to our country."

"It's okay, as long as we're together," she said. She kissed him tenderly. "I'm going to explore now. I think you can hear me call from anywhere in the room. And yes, I'll be careful."

"You read my mind," Plume said, smiling.

Ova swung on the vine and shinnied down it with ease. What a strange place the jungle corner was. No insects or creatures. No hot sun to make her sweat.

Idyllic in every way. Ova played in the jungle, examining leaves and branches to her heart's delight, until her heel slipped on a slick leaf and she plummeted down, too surprised to call out. She landed with a *thump,* on top of some type of structure, which she examined with great interest.

A large fence joined the ceiling and floor together and she slid down a bar in the fence until she hit ground. A huge gate stood before her, fastened with a latch. Ova pulled and prodded the giant latch until it clicked up and the white gate coasted open. Did animals live in here? No birds. No frogs or crickets. No fish in the pool. How strange.

Ova wandered about with small, hesitant steps, absorbing the strange place, smelling the beautiful blooms. Decorations of various sorts and sizes gave it an outdoor garden feel, but a strange sense of foreboding filled the air. As she approached the back of the garden, her nose wrinkled at an offensive odor, one she didn't like.

Leaves rustled, although there was no breeze. A tree trembled as something brushed by, and two green eyes peered through the leaves.

Ova opened her mouth to scream, but no sound came out.

The green eyes opened bigger, and a giant head surfaced above the tree.

Ova backed away, running her hand down the fence, feeling, praying to find the gate. Once more, she tried to scream, and placed a hand over her silent mouth. Plume! She must call Plume.

The huge head raised higher and higher, and the creature began crashing through the foliage, smashing trees and shrubs.

Ova picked up a decorative stone and beat it against the fence, hoping to disturb Plume's dreams, but the monster disliked the sound and loosed a mighty roar that made her fall backwards.

Drool filled its mouth and pink slobbers dripped to the ground as it approached. Its mouth opened to reveal jagged teeth that could easily rip Ova in half. The giant beast seemed to fill the whole place as it stretched a long green neck and plodded toward her, switching the air with a long red, split tongue that flicked closer to her with every step.

Ova's eyes grew to their largest proportion. *I am completely and utterly lost,* she thought. Her hand reached behind her and located the gate opening. She fought the blackness that threatened to envelop her. And then came the sweetest sound she had ever heard.

"Ova? Ova! Answer me," Plume said. "Where are you?"

His voice offered hope, but she dare not yell. Fighting to hold a steady and calm tone that would not disturb the beast, she said, "Plume. Help me. I'm straight down from you, and… you better hurry." She swallowed hard. "This beast thinks I am his dinner."

"Stay calm. I'm coming."

Plume slid down a long vine, and spotted Ova by the gate. His eyes caught sight of the monster's feet, and his eyes followed the green stocky legs all the way up to its long neck and devilish eyes. Now it stood very close, leering down at his meal. It reared on its hind feet, pitched his head back and loosed a thunderous roar.

Plume placed his arms under Ova's and pulled her outside the gate, whispering in her ear, "Move back very quietly and with as little movement as possible. I've got you. You'll be okay. Back… back. Don't scream. Don't cry. Okay, you're out now. Rise slowly and help me shut the big gate on that thing."

The monster bellowed once more, and reared.

Ova's eyes bulged.

Sweat formed on her brow.

Fear squeezed until she could barely breathe.

Hands slick with sweat.

Mouth so dry she couldn't scream.

"Now!" Plume yelled as the monster followed. "Close the gate!" The beast's head protruded through the doorway, but they pushed with all their might.

The gate slammed with such force that it

punched the creature's snout and it raged.

Plume pulled the latch down and the creature was trapped.

The two miniatures stood shivering, holding one another, backing away from the bellowing beast.

"I thought I had lost you," Plume said, stroking her hair.

"I thought you had, too."

"What is that thing?" he said.

"It must be Gordeen. I've heard the name, but have never seen it. Nor do I want to see it again," she said. "Shazar almost lost one of his pets tonight."

"*Two* of his pets. I would have fought to the death for you."

Heavy footsteps approached in the hall.

Plume and Ova crossed the room and sat where Shazar had left them, huddling together. The door opened, then closed.

"Come, Noids," Shazar said, putting a hand down. "I wanted you to play and explore and have fun while I was gone, but you have waited the whole time, bored, no doubt. We must work harder on communicating."

Ova and Plume climbed onto his hand, gestured with their appendages and rattled non-stop about their experience, but Shazar just laughed. "You are very excited tonight. Perhaps you are happy I have returned. Yes, that must be it." And he put them to bed for the night.

Over the course of the next season, Shazar and the Noids worked harder on communication skills. By the end of two seasons, they could hold bits of conversations.

Shazar set new records of achievement as a junior space pilot, contributing suggestions to the space program and using every opportunity to sharpen his skills. Maturity and leadership skills blossomed and flourished.

Plume and Ova pushed themselves to the limit to learn his language, and by the end of their tenth season with him, they were prepared for an in-depth meeting. When the giant entered the room, the Noids ran to meet him.

"Come, Noids," Shazar said, hand extended, and they jumped on.

"Shazar, we need to speak with you."

"You are doing so now," he said.

"We want to talk about something very important," Ova said.

"Speak on. I always have time for you."

Now 20-years old, the spaceship captain sat on the floor and perched the Noids on one knee. "But first, I must tell you something. Nothing has made me so happy as having you two. The day I first saw you, I knew you were very intelligent, so I devoted myself to training you. Look at your medals on the wall! You have won so many Noid contests, and I am very proud of you. I am no longer a boy, and I will be marrying in my twenty-first season. It is customary to give Noids away before the wedding, but I cannot. I want you to come live with us. I like this thing you call love! It swells my heart and gives me strength to face my fears. Without you--what would I do?"

Plume and Ova looked at one another.

"Now, what did you want to speak about?" Shazar said.

They looked at one another again. "You have never asked who or what we are or where we came from," Plume said. "Why is that?"

Shazar shrugged. "Because I know. You are Noids and you came from the pet shop."

"But before you found us at the pet shop, we lived at another place."

"I know about your first owner and how they split you up."

"No, before that, we lived on another planet."

"Where?" Shazar sat straighter, in rapt attention.

"Far away. Our world has been at war many seasons, and only a few thousand of us remain. Our soil is toxic and the food it produces is poisonous. Even the fish are toxic, so food is scarce, and many kill for it."

"But how did you get here?"

"Slavers captured us," they said in unison.

"Slavers? But that cannot be. Our forefathers outlawed slavery thousands of years ago." A deep furrow crinkled his brow.

"The slavers see us as domestic pets, and in all probability, have no idea how intelligent we are. We just speak a different language," Ova said.

"My people call you Noids," Shazar said. "What do you call yourselves?"

"*Noids* is a shortened term, taken from the word *humanoids.* We call ourselves *humans,* and the name of our planet is *Earth.*"

Shazar set them down, stood, and paced the floor. "I suppose you want to go home."

"We used to want that for many seasons," Plume said, "but now we have a better plan."

"Say on," Shazar said.

"You could put an end to slavery by bringing it to the attention of your justice system. Then you could collect all the Noids and build a little village for us, so we can be together. We miss our own kind. Having our own village would almost be like living on Earth. If you were to do that, we would want to have offspring, and the humanoid population would grow."

"You can have offspring? But... you haven't."

"We didn't want to raise a child in slavery. Shazar, you don't have to *own* us," Ova said. "We *want* to stay. We will be happy to have offspring and work in the crop fields. We are not toys. We are a hard-working people, and without our work, we have no purpose. No reason for being."

"A humanoid village? Offspring? Work in the fields? What an amazing idea! You could set up your own government and live independently..." Sadness crossed his face and he looked away. "But I would miss you."

"Not if you move your wife to a large property and build the village there," Ova said.

"And if I do this, you will have little ones? And they will be mine?"

"We call them *babies*, or *children*, and they will belong to the maters and paters who bear them, like you belong to yours," Plume said. "If we had a village, we could live a dignified life, and we could still be together any time we wish."

Strange, wet things slid down Shazar's purple face, tickling as it went. He brushed it with his fourth hand and looked at the wetness on his fingers. "I leak?" he said.

"No, my friend," Plume said. "You are crying. That is a good thing. It means you understand what love is."

Shazar held Plume and Ova up to his face and gave them a tiny squeeze as they wiped his tears.

"You need your freedom. My people need to learn about love. We are good for each other. Tell me how to build a village."

* * *

BIO: Deborah Owen is the CEO and founder of Creative Writing Institute. CWI provides a variety of writing courses with personal tutors and is a nonprofit charity that offers free writing courses to cancer survivors. Deborah won Honorable Mention over 16,000 entries in a Writer's Digest short story contest and has had many articles accepted for publication. She loves God, her family and Kettle potato chips.

Details
by Jianna Higgins
Head Judge & Award Winning Author

It was like staring up at Judge Judy in her courtroom except two judges stood on separate podiums. The angel wore a dazzling white robe surrounded by golden brilliance. The demon wore black, and orange flames licked at the air around him.

Lizzie's eyes swiveled between them and as three questions collided, she blurted, "Who are you? Where am I? What happened?" A low mist slunk across the entire floor and swallowed her feet.

The male gave her a toothy grin. "I'll start. You are Elizabeth Abbott and I am Levi, your reaper. You died. Remember?"

It took half a second to remember driving along the highway, bopping her head to something on the car radio. Her last conscious moment included a blur rocketing toward her in her left peripheral vision. As she turned her head, she saw the stop sign the other driver hadn't. Then it hit. T-boned. Door crumpled. Glass shattered. Bones broken. Oblivion.

Lizzie gulped. "What is this? A competition for my soul?" The golden ceiling sparkled like a million tiny suns, and golden cherubs hung from the roof. Long, narrow windows, six inches deep, ran along the top of each wall. Silvery sunbeams slanted down into the murky fog like a waterslide from Heaven to Hell.

The female's smile lit her face and she nodded. "Bang on. I'm Sophia, and I'm determined to be your reaper, although I think it might be an uphill battle. What do you think?"

Lizzie wanted to say, *no, I'm yours*, but memories popped up of mean things she'd said or done, and she held her tongue. Angels probably knew what she'd done before she knew it herself. The ground suddenly lurched sideways as if to shake her out of her thoughts. She reached for something to grab onto, but her arms found only empty air. She righted herself and felt unseen hands that dragged at her legs, pulling down, down.

Levi snapped his fingers and the pulling stopped. "Sorry about that. Look, I'm the fun guy here," he said. "Choose me, and we'll have a great time together."

Lizzie's eyes raked over Levi's delicious olive skin and black, sparkling eyes. Totally hot. Although cold air snaked around her legs, heat from his flames caressed Lizzie's face. Born during a winter snow storm, she disliked hot weather and assumed Hell would not be a comfortable place to live forever.

"Where's the other driver?"

"That was a no brainer." Levi flicked his eyebrows up and down for Sophia's benefit. "She was mine from the moment puberty hit."

Lizzie's dry mouth tasted like bird seed. She placed a hand on her chest to calm herself but nothing beat beneath her fingers. Dead? Was that the reason for the constant ringing in her ears? A death knell?

"So how come *I* get to choose?"

"You're a half and half," Levi said.

"Huh?"

Sophia interrupted. "There's equal good and bad in you, which is very rare, so neither of us is the clear winner. From this moment forward, we'll give you seven days to make your choice."

"I get to live another week? Why can't I choose now?" Lizzie believed in God, but she had dark thoughts about punishing the people who hurt her.

"It doesn't work like that," Levi said. "You're going to wake up in the hospital, and the best part is you won't remember this conversation. We're going to judge you on what you think, what you say, how you behave. I'm just thankful you're far from boring."

Images of one very large fiery pit invaded her mind. "I thought you said I'd get to choose where I go," she said in a panic.

Levi wagged a long slim finger at her. "God gave you free will. That's where your choice lies."

Sophia added, "How you proceed in the next week will determine your everlasting life. In seven days we'll meet back here, and I hope to win your soul."

Lizzie clenched her fists, hoping her long fingernails would cut into her skin and wake her from this nightmare. She felt nothing but the tingling in her nose from the musty stench of sulphur. Her feet seemed glued to the floor, and she couldn't lift them. She swallowed hard. "What will I die of in seven days?"

Levi answered as he inspected his fingernails.

"Unexpected complications. See you soon."

~ * ~

Lizzie opened her eyes. The first thing that registered was pain that radiated down her left side from her brain to her toes. A blood pressure cuff tightened around her right bicep and sounded like a long, loud hiss as it took a reading. "Wh... where am I? What happened?" The words came out in a crackled whisper.

A nurse in salmon scrubs held a stethoscope in the crook of Lizzie's arm. "Welcome back, Lizzie. You've been in a car accident, and you're in the hospital. Your blood pressure is a little high, but it'll come down once you're up and about. How do you feel?"

"Like I wish I was dead. I hurt. Everywhere. I need drugs."

The nurse removed the cuff and pressed two fingers against Lizzie's wrist. "You're due for another shot of morphine in two hours. You'll have to wait till then."

"Two hours? No. I can't wait. I'm dying from the pain here. Give me something."

The nurse wrote on a chart. "You have a broken arm, a broken collar bone, and you've got concussion, but you aren't dying. I'll let the doctor know you're awake." She pointed to the bed next to Lizzie where a full body cast encased a sleeping woman. "You should think yourself lucky." She left the room.

"But I feel like a truck ran over me," she croaked. A different nurse entered the room to check the vitals of the woman in the next bed, and Lizzie slitted her eyes to pretend she was still asleep.

The nurse left the blood pressure machine at the end of the bed and looked at her with sympathy. "You need the sleep," she whispered. "I'll leave your medicine here and help you take it when you wake up."

Lizzie's ears pricked up. *Pills? Steal them?* she thought, but then shook her head. *No!* A second thought shouted, *Two more hours! I can't stand this. I can't.*

Using her right arm, she pushed herself up to sitting as throbbing pain pounded down her left side. Dizzy, she waited a moment before placing her right foot on the floor before testing weight on the left.

Though bruised and swollen, it was bearable.

The small cup of pills sat innocently, and it was all she could see. Lizzie limped her way to the woman's nightstand and peered inside the paper cup. The round white tablet was definitely Oxycodone, but what were the others?

The young woman, with long fair hair that fanned her pillow, shifted her weight and the mattress creaked.

Lizzie froze, guilty, even though she had not acted on her thoughts.

The woman groaned, as if in pain, but didn't open her eyes.

Lizzie reached for the cup, tipped the contents into her mouth, grabbed a full cup of water on her nightstand and swallowed. Immediately, shame bloomed in her cheeks.

The light in the room suddenly darkened as if an unknown force had consumed the sun. Just before the light returned to full brightness, laughter echoed in the walls.

Lizzie startled and glanced around the room. *Morphine delusion?* She hobbled back to bed, carefully slid under the covers and closed her eyes. Within twenty minutes the pain had backed off, and the edges of the world had a prism-like glow. She wanted to laugh at her chipped nail polish, at the undulating paint on the ceiling, at the pretty colors that looked like the inside of a kaleidoscope. Her heavy lids closed.

When she awoke, only faint lights glowed on the walls. Curtains covered the windows. She felt hung over.

An unfamiliar nurse arrived and placed her hands on her hips. Through tight lips she said, "You stole Rosie's medication, didn't you? Then you were given morphine on top of it. You silly girl, you could have died."

Lizzie met the steely blue eyes. "It wasn't me. I can't get out of bed."

"We took bloods when you couldn't be roused. It *was* you."

Lizzie shrugged and closed her eyes. At least the pain only roared in the distance. She heard the nurse's shoes squelch across the floor and disappear down the corridor.

A sickly voice came from the other bed. "You stole my medicine. Couldn't you tell how much I needed it? They wouldn't give me any more for a long time."

Lizzie turned to her fully-awake neighbor. *Uh oh. Time to face the music.* "I'm really sorry. You were asleep, and I couldn't think past my own pain. Are you okay?"

"Are you kidding? No, I'm not okay. How could you do that?"

Lizzie decided a defense was pointless. "So, what happened to you? Something epic, right?"

The woman's hazel eyes blazed with fury. "Epic? Seriously? I was pushing my one year old daughter in a stroller across a pedestrian crossing when a drunk driver slammed into us."

"Whoa, that's terrible. You're a bit busted up, huh?"

Cuts on Rosie's face and hands glowed an angry red. "Both arms, both legs and my pelvis are broken. My little girl's in a coma in pediatric intensive care, and I can't go to her."

Lizzie sucked her thumbnail as guilt clawed at

her throat. She closed her eyes and imagined fear probably outweighed physical pain. "I'm sorry, okay? Really sorry."

Rosie huffed and turned away. "The Bible says to love everyone. Sometimes it's not easy. Apology noted. Acceptance is pending."

Lizzie stared at the ceiling and wished words of wisdom were written up there. As soon as she heard long, even breaths from Rosie's bed, she knew she had to make it right. Lizzie slipped out of bed, paused at the doorway and peeked down the corridor.

Clear.

Hearing voices in the room across the hall, she flattened herself against the wall and listened.

A doctor spoke with authority. "This orderly is going to take you up to theater now. You aren't allergic to morphine? No? Good. I see you brought your own medication with you. What is it?"

"Oxycodone," a woman said.

"We'll put those away in your drawer, and you can take them home with you. While you're here in the hospital, you must only take medication that is prescribed by me."

Lizzie heard a muffled voice and then the doctor spoke again.

"If all goes well, your spinal fusion will be fully healed in six to nine months, and you will no longer require pain medication. Right, orderly, you may take Mrs. Davis now. The anesthesiologist is waiting for her."

Lizzie glanced up and down the corridor but didn't make a decision fast enough.

The bed eased out of the room and the orderly turned it toward a bank of elevators. The doctor and a younger man in a white coat marched behind in single file.

No one noticed Lizzie in a hospital gown hugging the wall.

Once the group entered the elevator, Lizzie backed into the vacated room. Keeping one ear out for advancing footsteps, she reached into the top drawer and wrapped a hand around a bottle of pills. Oxycodone. Yes! A little bottle of magic.

Halfway back to the door, a vice clamped around Lizzie's heart.

Sure, the woman would have medication

prescribed while in the hospital, but what about when she returned home?

Take half and leave the rest? Good idea. And then she heard footsteps approaching and a rattling trolley. Lizzie shuffled over to the door and stood behind it, not breathing.

"Now where's Elizabeth Abbott gone? Check the bathroom."

"Not here. Would she leave the building?"

"No idea, but we'd better find her before the end of our shift."

The voices faded away.

Lizzie examined the bottle in her hand. Hurry. Using her mouth and right hand, she removed the top and tipped half the contents onto the nightstand.

The tablets glared at her and she swallowed. "Okay, okay," she muttered, and returned all but two to the bottle.

Back in her room, Lizzie placed one tablet in an empty meds cup and hid it in Rosie's drawer in case of an emergency. She left the other one in her pocket. About to slip into bed, she paused, sighed, reached into her pocket and placed the second tablet in Rosie's paper cup as well.

Lizzie gripped the rail on her bed and stopped to think. She hadn't done enough. What could she do to cheer up Rosie? She hobbled into the single room next door and peered around.

A middle-aged woman occupied one of the beds. Her perfectly styled silver hair contrasted against her sunken cheeks and grey pallor.

Lizzie pulled open the drawer of the nightstand and found an unopened block of Caramello chocolate. *Rosie might like that,* she thought and reached toward it.

The woman opened her eyes. "Are you a habitual thief, or just an opportunist?"

"What? No. I... it's not for me. It's for my roommate. She's in a really bad way. I thought it would make her feel better."

"Go ahead, take it. I'm a diabetic anyway." Her dark brown eyes bore into Lizzie. "I sense so much good in you. Why are you a thief?"

Lizzie pursed her lips. "I don't know. My mother always said I was full of the devil."

The woman drew in a slow breath as she

continued to scrutinize Lizzie. "She may be right. Do something about that, okay?" Her body shuddered and she winced. "Now please excuse me. Dying is a painful and tiring occupation."

"Thank you for the candy. I hope you get to feeling better," she said, even though it seemed pointless.

Back in her room, Lizzie noted Rosie's soft, even breathing. She laid the chocolate within easy reach of Rosie's hand and climbed into her own bed.

Did I do the right thing, she thought. *Maybe I should keep the pills. Yeah, and the chocolate in case I need them.* She heard a gentle voice inside her head say, 'Trust.' Too tired to argue with her insanity, she sank into her pillow. As she drifted off to sleep, she heard a whispered conversation out in the corridor.

"She was on a mission to steal, Sophia."

"Look, Levi, I realize she struggles to do the right thing, but I feel her desire to change."

"Sophia, you're so naïve. Stop trying to see the good in people when there isn't any."

"No, Levi, you're missing the finer details here."

Sophia? Levi? Who were they? Lizzie had a

vague recollection of meeting two people with those names. Were they medical students who followed the doctor like sheep and talked about her as if she were a prime rib roast? She wished the staff would remember their patients needed sleep to heal.

When Lizzie awoke, she felt a piece of paper in her curled-up right hand. Ignoring her useless left hand strapped inside a sling, she used her teeth to pull it open and found a typed message.

A personal message from god to the sinner elizabeth abbott: matthew 15:19 - For out of an evil heart comes theft.

Breathing became short and shallow, and her heart galloped inside her chest. Lizzie scanned the room. Where did the note come from? From God? But the message sounded right. For her own selfish comfort she had stolen Rosie's pain medication. She had followed up with further theft in neighboring rooms. Lizzie wanted to tear the paper into a thousand tiny fragments, but she needed two hands. Instead she crumpled it and threw it behind her head, heard it hit the wall and drop down behind the headboard.

Lizzie chewed her bottom lip as hopelessness

sank her deeper into the mattress. Drifting off to sleep again, she heard the same people talking in the hall and wished they would have more consideration.

"Levi, you can't just leave words out of Scriptures and scramble them to suit yourself. Look at the effect it's having on her."

"Come on, Sophia, you're surprised I don't play by the rules? Get over it."

"And God has a capital *G*."

"Not where I come from."

Extreme heat woke Lizzie. She slapped at the flames biting her legs and took three steps backward. The air smelled of burned and rotting flesh, and the sound of agonizing wails hung in the air.

Fat black snakes slithered through the grey mist that covered the floor. They reared their heads and hissed, forked tongues darting in and out.

"Welcome, Elizabeth, how do you like your eternal home? It's a bit of a fixer-upper, but we like it."

Lizzie couldn't locate the voice. She backed against a stone wall. Breathing too fast, the heat seared her throat muscles and vocal chords. Her mouth opened and closed, but nothing came out, while her heart thumped like a bongo drum.

With a whack, she landed back in her bed. A dream? Or was that Hell? To make matters worse, the couple were still arguing in the hallway.

"How did you do that? You're a cheat, Sophia."

"It's called realistic projection. I was just showing her what she'll escape if she leaves the dark side behind. I played by the rules, Levi."

"That gave you an unfair advantage, and I don't like it."

"Take it up with my boss. Oh, stop pouting."

When Lizzie woke, images suddenly began to play in her mind. She turned toward her neighbor. "Rosie, is your husband much taller than you?"

"Yes, why?"

"I just had a vision of you and him standing outside a small yellow house with white trim and window boxes. A little girl of about two stood beside you, and you're holding a baby wrapped in a blue blanket."

Rosie's face scrunched. "How could you know that? We only bought the house two weeks ago. I want to get window boxes, but we don't have any yet. And I'm definitely not pregnant. Kayla's only 12 months old and not expected to live. You're full of it."

"Sometimes I get these visions and they come true. I think your little girl will survive, and you're going to have a son in about a year."

"Leave me alone. The Bible says anything from a psychic comes from the devil, so what you just said is false testimony. Don't even talk to me." Rosie turned her face toward the wall.

"I wouldn't know what's in the Bible," Lizzie whispered as she fiddled with the bed cover. "And why did I think that would help her?"

She thought back to neighbors she'd had several years ago. The couple had adopted two mixed-race babies because Ted was unable to have children. When their marriage broke up, Raewyn decided her next husband would have dark skin so future offspring would look similar to her adopted children.

"You won't," Lizzie had replied. "I saw a vision of you with two fair-skinned boys with white blonde hair."

A year later the neighbor remarried. Nine

months after that, Raewyn had the first of her two new blonde-haired sons.

Confusion sizzled through Lizzie's brain. Raewyn was a Christian and one of the godliest women she knew. Her neighbor later admitted the message gave her hope for the future and lifted her depression.

This gift was from the devil? Why would he tell her something so good? Clearly he'd had an ulterior motive, and Lizzie had played into his hands. A deep aching depression settled over her and she eventually fell asleep.

An hour later, she woke with another crumpled paper in her hand. Holding her breath, she read the typed words.

From god to the sinner elizabeth abbott: leviticus 20:27 - A man or woman who is a psychic shall surely be put to death. They shall be stoned to death; their blood shall be upon them.

She wanted to eat the paper to remove the evidence because the accusation was true. Fear snaked up her spine and over her skin. God was clearly angry, and He should be. It was unnatural to know things before they happen. The fingers of her right hand curled as anger seeped through her body and her nails dug into the stiff white bed sheet.

Rosie's nurse entered with an overly-bright smile plastered on her face. "Your daughter has woken up. I couldn't wait to tell you!"

Rosie scrambled to try and sit up before remembering she couldn't move. "My baby woke up? That means she'll be all right, doesn't it?"

The smile slipped from the nurse's face. "Well, she has internal bleeding, but keep thinking positive thoughts."

"I have to go to her. Please. You have to help me."

"You can't be moved from women's surgical to pediatric ICU. Cross infection."

Lizzie shuddered. Bureaucracy could slap people so hard it left welts of betrayal.

After a nap, Lizzie woke to soft sobbing in the bed next to her and then realized another piece of paper lay in her hand.

From god to the sinner elizabeth abbott: colossians 3:5: - You will be put to death for your earthly nature: sexual immorality, impurity, lust, evil desires, greed, idolatry. Because of those, the wrath of god is coming upon you.

Lizzie could tick every sin on the list. Maybe the car accident was God's wrath, and her pain was the penance followed by eternity in Hell. "Yes, I get it. I deserve this punishment. Since I'm going to Hell anyway, I'm gonna do something to fix what I did to Rosie." But being broken on one side of her body limited her options.

She lay staring at the ceiling, waiting for the answer. A gun! She could force a nurse to take Rosie to her daughter. No. Couldn't do it. Even pretending she could hurt others crushed her lungs. Hopelessness set in and anger seethed.

What else?

As a minor author of teenage fiction who floated in a sea amongst huge names, Lizzie had some powerful friends on Facebook. *I know. What if I...? No, that's just stupid.* But Colleen Hoover, a world famous young adult author, was often responsive. *She probably gets 10,000 messages an hour, but I have to try.* Lizzie used her phone to send a text on the

Messenger app.

Now what?

Pray?

The thought brought tears to her eyes at her betrayal of the God she had loved as a child.

How about phoning the governor or a congressman? She laughed out loud and then winced as new waves of pain down shot down the left side.

Two hours later, a nurse and an orderly zoomed into the room. "Rosie! You're being moved so you can be with your daughter. Some famous book writer contacted the hospital CEO and insisted he cut the red tape. Lucky you, having friends in high places!"

Did I do that? Lizzie checked her phone and found a text from Colleen Hoover that said, "Done," followed by a smiley face. About to tell Rosie that it was she who had set this turn of events in motion and perhaps elicit forgiveness, a text pinged onto her phone from someone called Sophia.

Be careful not to practice your righteousness before other people in order to be seen by them, for then you will have no reward from your Father who is in Heaven. Matthew 6:1.

Lizzie's hand shook and she dropped her phone on the bed. As Rosie's bed rumbled out into the corridor, she picked it up again and looked for Sophia's message. The last message showing was from Colleen Hoover. She shook her head and shut the phone off. *I'm losing it*, she thought.

Outside, grey clouds hung low and sullen, and trees whipped around in a frenzy that matched her mood.

Fingers of light were creeping into the room when Lizzie woke again, and despair rushed through her. "I am completely and utterly lost," she whispered. When she rubbed a hand over her sleepy eyes, a piece of paper dropped onto her chest and she gulped. She flicked it to the floor, but it flew back up and landed beside her hand. Clearly it wouldn't be ignored.

From God to his beloved child Elizabeth Abbott: Psalm 103:8 - The Lord is merciful and gracious, slow to anger and abounding in steadfast love.

Lizzie lowered her eyes to think about the words. This message was different to previous ones and she tingled with warmth. When she looked back at the paper, the words had changed.

From God to his beloved child Elizabeth Abbott: Jeremiah 29:11: - For I know the plans I have for you, declares the Lord. Plans to prosper you and not to harm you, plans to give you hope and a future.

Lizzie's eyes brimmed, and she raised her eyes to the ceiling. "God, I'm sorry for all the bad things I've done and how I've disappointed you." But the feelings of wretchedness seeped away, and peace settled over her heart as she fell asleep again.

Later, while a nurse took Lizzie's temperature and blood pressure, she said, "I forgot to tell you. Rosie asked me to give you a message. *Apology accepted.*"

Lizzie nodded and a tear escaped. "How is her daughter?"

"She's doing really well. They both are. It's a miracle really."

On the seventh day after the car accident, Lizzie woke with her left temple pulsing. "Nurse," she said, "can I please have some Tylenol? My head hurts."

"I'll check with the doctor when he arrives. He's in surgery right now."

Lizzie's brain felt like it was inside a crusher

while a shimmering aura coated her vision. She wanted to block the intrusive light but couldn't move. She tried to call for help again, but she fell into a tunnel where darkness became more and more pervasive. Her bed moved for several minutes, stopped, and moved again. She heard people speaking close to her bed.

"It's a subdural hematoma on the left frontal lobe, close to a major artery. Get her into surgery, stat. And someone should call her family if she has any."

A younger voice responded, "Will she make it?"

Hesitation. The older man spoke again. "I don't know, but even if she does, she's almost certain to face personality changes, loss of motor skills and language, impaired judgement."

A young female voice spoke, "She already showed poor judgment by driving drunk."

"The drunk driver died at the scene. This one's the innocent party."

"Oh, I didn't know, sorry. I thought she was responsible. What happens now?"

The voices faded.

~ * ~

Lizzie awoke--back in the courtroom. Memories returned of meeting Sophia and Levi and the prophecy of her death. Would Saint Peter meet her outside the gates? Were they actually pearly? Or how quickly would she land in Hell, the land of the lost, the condemned, the unforgiven?

The angel and demon stared at her.

Lizzie straightened and tried to hide her quivering hands. "When will it happen? Will it hurt when I get to Hell? Will I be covered in flesh-melting burns forever?" Bile rose in her throat along with the fear. All her past deeds flashed before her eyes. She made no effort to conceal the tears that coursed down her cheeks. *I did whatever I wanted, and it's cost me a peaceful eternity. If only I'd known, because the cost is too high.*

"You sure have been fun to follow these past seven days," Levi said, leering at her. "Just one more day and I'm sure…"

"Hey, I heard you two talking near my room. I just remembered."

"You did? That's not supposed to happen," Sophia said.

Levi stared at Lizzie as if she suddenly had three heads. "Whoa, that's scary. Very few people know when we're around, let alone can hear us."

The angel interrupted. "Elizabeth, your score after the bonus seven days came out at 52:48. I won, but only just."

Lizzie's mouth dropped open. Not going to Hell? "What about all the Scriptures that God put in my hand? He's so mad at me."

Sophia shook her head. "Not so. Levi has a way of twisting Scriptures to make them hateful. The last few were from me, and they were direct quotes."

Lizzie chewed on her thumbnail as she processed the information. "But I'm evil. I'm a psychic. That's supposed to be bad, right?"

"No, Elizabeth. God gave you the gift of discernment. You use it to help others, not to make a profit off of other people's misery. Yes, you've been a challenge, but God loves you very much."

"He loves me? Why, after everything I've done?"

"In the book of Ephesians it states, 'But God, rich in mercy, because of the great love for us, even when we were dead in transgressions, made us alive again together in Christ--by God you have been saved.' So, even though you've sinned, God wants you by his side. The only issue is… you haven't given your life over to Christ."

"I don't understand."

"No one can enter Heaven without asking Jesus into their heart. Once you're dead, it's too late."

Confusion clouded Lizzie's brain. "You won my soul, but I can't go to Heaven because it's too late? Where does that leave me?" Her mouth felt so dry she couldn't swallow. "Can I make an appointment with God and negotiate a deal?"

Sophia clutched her stomach and laughed. "The answer is no. But you aren't dead yet. Your body is still on the operating table in V-Fib. The surgeon is trying to stabilize you."

"I'm not… dead? But I'm going to be, right?"

Sophia shook her head and smiled. "Here's my gift to you… I've negotiated an open-ended life-contract for you with God because you show so much desire to change. Don't ask me when you'll die. Only the big guy in the sky knows the answer."

Levi's eyes widened, and he scanned the room. "Are you allowed to say stuff like that?"

"Oh, you're scared? Good for you, Levi." She made an X with two fingers. "And yes, God and I are like this."

Lizzie faced the demon. "Gutted much?" Whoops, it probably wasn't okay to gloat, even to a demon. She tapped fingers against her chin and grinned. "Sorry, Levi. Maybe I should say, how do you feel about that?"

Levi looked unperturbed. "Hey, your Date of Birth and Date of Death are merely details. Since you're not dying yet, you still have time to mess up, which means I still have a chance to win your soul. And I will. I'm very skilled at whispering bad ideas into people's ears."

Sophia shook her head again. "Don't listen to him, Lizzie. He won't have a chance if you choose to give your life to Jesus."

Lizzie gazed into the angel's face, full of love and acceptance, and at the handsome Levi whose narrowed eyes and scowling smirk oozed hate. "You're not getting my soul, Levi. I know I'll mess up, but God loves me. For the first time, I understand forgiveness. I'll praise Him for the rest of my life for giving me a second chance at life, and I don't just mean that I'm still breathing. I repent. Is that the right word?" When Sophia nodded, she added, "I never want to disappoint God again. Like, ever!"

Sophia's face glowed with love. "If you want to send Levi packing forever, you must ask Jesus into your heart. Are you ready to do that?"

Lizzie nodded and repeated Sophia's words. "Jesus, I ask you to be my Lord and Savior, to forgive my sins and save me from eternal separation from God. I accept your death on the cross as payment for my sins. Thank you for providing a way for me to have a relationship with my heavenly Father. Through faith in you, I have eternal life. Please help me to walk in your will. Amen."

"How do you feel?" Sophia asked.

Lizzie touched fingers to her wet cheeks. "Why am I crying when I've never felt so happy... or so loved?"

"God's love just poured into your heart through the Holy Spirit. You'll never be the same again."

Levi vanished into thin air. No fanfare. No billowing smoke. Gone.

* * *

BIO: Jianna is the author of the multi-award winning Sorrento series and she is currently writing the first book in the Silver Sleuth series. Jianna's books have won First Place in the Book Excellence Awards, First Place in the LYRA Book Awards, two Gold medals, two Silver medals and an Honorable Mention medal in the Global Ebook Awards, an Honorable Mention medal and three Finalist medals in the Readers' Favorite International Book Awards. Jianna is a Kiwi who loves chocolate, supporting the NZ All Blacks rugby team and sliding on snow.

http://jiannahiggins.com/

Arpie
by S. Joan Popek
Judge, CWI Staff & Award Winning Author

Doctor Gertrude Habershaw watched her masterpiece floating behind the glass plating.

Hundreds of mirrors positioned at all angles and reflected every aspect of his three-hundred-pound frame. He stretched out to his full length with steel-alloy arms and legs floating straight out from his body, bright red eyes staring at the myriad reflections.

The wires leading from his oval head and square chest to an unseen point in the mirrored ceiling fed vast quantities of information to his internal processing unit at the speed of light.

"Is his education finished?" Habershaw said into the microphone on the table in front of her. She leaned forward with both palms flat against the table, her face almost touching the glass she watched through. These two minuscule actions betrayed to no one but herself how excited she was. To the other two people in the room, she appeared calm and even a little bit bored.

"Just a few more seconds," Harry's voice replied into her earpiece. "There, it's done. Just fed him the last of it."

She glanced up at the husky man sitting in the

glass case perched above the floating robot and nodded. "Okay, lower him down. Let's see if all these months' work was worth it."

Harry smiled and bent over his microphone, "Okay. Let's see if this baby can sing!"

Slowly the cables extended until the robot's feet touched the floor. The cables released and withdrew into the mirrored ceiling. Robot Prototype-10-series 1143, RP-10 as the team had been calling him, stood motionless and surveyed the three human forms behind the window with unblinking red eyes.

Habershaw took a deep breath and keyed the sealed door. It slid open silently, and she stood on the threshold a moment before entering the chamber. If her theories were correct, the world's first robot capable of true independent thinking had just been born. She was on edge as she approached it. If anything was wrong with her calculations, they would soon know.

It turned to face her with a grace that belied its bulk and stood at least three feet taller than she. "Mother?" it said, in a somewhat metallic but clear voice.

Habershaw stopped dead still. "What?"

"Are you my Mother?"

"Your...? Of course not," she snapped, ignoring the muffled giggles from her crew just outside the door. Suddenly she turned to face them. "Okay, whose idea of a joke is this? It's not funny. This is a multi-million-dollar investment, and it's not something to joke around with."

The giggles ceased as quickly as they had begun, and the two engineers, Gordon and Jonas, stood shaking their heads in quick denial.

Harry joined them. He shrugged his ample shoulders and said, "Aww--come on doctor Habershaw, you know none of us would do something so stupid as to tinker with that thing. We know what you'd do to us if we did. Nope, I believe it really thinks you are its mama." He shrugged again. "I mean, we did build him to think."

Habershaw turned back to the robot. "No, RP-10. I am not your... your mother." She ignored the muffled giggles behind her. "I am, however, your creator."

"You are God?"

"No! I'm a scientist, and you are RP-10, a robot. A very special robot."

"I am Arpie Ten? That is my name?"
"No. Not Arpie. You are RP."

"Very well." The robot nodded. "I am Arpie." He placed his three-fingered hand to his chest, stood silent as the red lights that were his eyes flashed red and green alternately. When they settled back into the ruby glow, he nodded. "Yes, Arpie will do fine. Everyone has a name, you know." It turned and surveyed the room and the three humans outside the door, then turned back to Habershaw. "Well, if you are not my mother, where is she?"

"I told you. You don't have a mother. You are a robot--a machine--that we built."

"We?"

"Us--all of us." She waved her hand in a semi-circle to encompass the group now just inside the door.

"But everyone has a mother. Logic demands it." He turned to the grinning group at the door. "Do you know where my mother is?"

No one spoke. Finally, Harry raised his hand and pointed at Habershaw. "Guess we might as well start with the basics. If you did have a mother, I suppose it would be her." He struggled to hide the amused smirk that appeared on his face, but lost the battle and covered his mouth with a hand, pretending to cough.

Jonas turned to Gordon. "Gordon, you didn't, like, cut any corners, did you?"

"Uh, no, uh--not really."

Gertrude spun around. "What do you mean, *not really*?"

"Well, I--uh--I just thought we could speed things up a bit if I left a few basics out."

Jonas ran his fingers through his hair. Static electricity immediately pulled the sparse covering straight up, making it look more like an emaciated shock of wheat that waved gently. "Oh, not again! What *basics*?"

"What *basics*?" Habershaw echoed.

"Um--well--just the details of his--uh--creation. You know the specifics of robotic circuitry." He grinned sheepishly and stared at Habershaw. "I mean, you did build him as the first AI, the first artificial intelligence with the ability to actually think and learn. You were in a hurry, so I just figured he could pick up the specifics by learning them. I mean, if he's truly capable of independent thinki--"

"*Excuse* me!" Arpie's metallic voice rang out. "I am right here, you know. I can *hear* you." His voice had a definite hint of pout in it. "It's not polite to talk about people when they are in the room. In fact, it's not polite to talk about people at all unless you have something good to say." He looked at Habershaw. "Isn't that right, Mother?"

"I am not your mother! And you are not *people*! How many times do I have to...? Never mind. Just stay here for a minute." She glared at Gordon, then turned to Harry. "Harry, watch him a minute. You two!" She gestured Gordon and Jonas. "Come with me." She stalked off toward her office at a stiff-shouldered

- 112 -

military pace.

The two followed meekly. Jonas punched Gordon in the ribs and whispered, "How many times do I have to tell you, don't cut corners?"

"I didn't think it would hurt," he whispered back. "After all, the old biddy was in such a hurry..." A glare from Habershaw standing at her doorway silenced him.

"Get in there, you two screw-ups."

They got.

Habershaw shut the door and strode to the window. "Do you know what you've done?"

Gordon swallowed the lump in his throat. "Well, I... um..."

"Shut up, moron."

"Yes, Ma'am."

Jonas took a hesitant step forward. "Look, Doctor Habershaw, there's no need to call this idiot names." He pointed to Gordon. "I mean after all..." Her venomous look chased the rest of his sentence to a blank. To heck with protecting Gordon. This was an 'every man for himself' moment. He took back the brave step forward in retreat.

The rest of the conversation went something like this: "Imbeciles--morons--incompetent over the hill fools! Fix it!" The tirade ended with a not so veiled threat to send them to the furthest, coldest, darkest galaxy outpost she could find if they failed.

Out in the hall, Jonas ran his fingers through his hair. "How could you do this to me? Any technical engineer with half a brain could follow the schematics and get the knowledge base right."

"Hey, no need to yell," Gordon said. "We can fix this. Just a matter of reprogramming, that's all."

Jonas' face turned bright red. "We? We? *We* didn't get us into this mess. *You* did. Just like you did the Terra-4-U robot. Only I don't think this one will be as easy to fix. That was just a glorified tractor. This is an…"

Gordon frowned. "AI. I know. So, it's a little more complicated, that's all. At least he doesn't think he's listening to the voice of God like Terra-4-U did. You know I always thought…"

Jonas stared at Gordon. "I don't care what you thought. And have you forgotten that you can't reprogram a cybernetic brain? It's not all metal and circuit boards, you know. We're talking integrated circuitry and neuro-stimulated cells and neural interfaces. He's part cybernetic, part electronic and part guesswork. You can't just upload data," he said, waving one arm. "He's past that since the electronic education process is over. We could really screw up the information he already has. No, we can't take the chance. Now, he must gain additional information in the old-fashioned way--by learning. That's how we built him. That's why he's AI. Aww, you know that." Jonas frowned. "Come on, let's go see what we can do for Arpie. Once more, *I* have to save our behinds." He ran his fingers through his hair and stalked toward the lab.

Gordon followed at a slower pace. "What's he doing?" Gordon asked Harry when they entered the lab.

The robot was sitting cross-legged on the floor, carefully examining every inch of his chest and mid-section of his square torso.

"We've been discussing the importance of the belly button. I suppose he's looking for his," Harry said. "He's really pretty amazing."

"Belly button?" Jonas said.

"Yeah, you know how everyone gets one when they're born. I was trying to explain he didn't really have a mama 'cause he wasn't really born. I thought if I told him about human babies, he'd get it."

"And?"

"He asked where his belly button is. I tried to explain it, but he's still looking."

"Great! Just what we need. The world's first super intelligent robot sitting on the floor playing with himself." Jonas glared at Gordon.

"Don't worry. I'll fix him," Gordon said. "It's

just a matter of looking at the schematics and putting a little thought into it."

"Yeah, well it better be," Jonas said with a growl.

Harry yawned. "Well, my work here is done. Think I'll go get some shut eye." He grinned. "I want to be plenty rested when the wicked witch lets you two have it for screwing up her pride and joy." He laughed and walked away whistling.

Gordon went over and bent over the robot. "Hey, Arpie. What'cha doin'?"

He raised his head and stared at Gordon with unblinking red eyes. "You know what I'm doing. I heard you talking about me like I wasn't even in the room. Rude. That's what you are. Rude." He unbent his legs and stood towering over the two men. "I can't seem to find my belly button." A soft whirring sound came from his chest, he slumped his shoulders and stared at the floor.

"What was that sound?" Jonas asked. "Why isn't he moving? Did you break him?"

Gordon shrugged his shoulders. "He sighed, or at least I think that's what it was. And no--I didn't break him. How could I? He weighs twice what I do. I hate to say this, but I think he's depressed about not having a belly button."

"*Depressed*? Robots don't get depressed. They

don't have feelings. You know that."

"Until now, they didn't." Gordon said. "This is an AI, remember? His neural networks and data mining make him capable of learning billions of associated concepts without relying on logical structures used by other robots. He may not feel pain, or bleed if you could cut his alloy exterior, but he still sees life as important, and he sees himself as being alive. After all, AI's are supposed to be imitations of us. Remember, we made him to be sentient."

"Well, yeah. Isn't that the point of artificial intelligence? To build a robot capable of reasoning?" Jonas shook his head. "So, what's your point?"

"Maybe being sentient means he has feelings, too."

Jonas sneered. "Feelings? That's just plain impossible. You know that." He glanced at the robot. "But... well... I suppose... well, if he *does* have feelings, we made one very big mistake. We'd better figure a way to fix it and make him forget his belly button or we're going to get awfully cold where Doctor Habershaw will send us." He turned to the robot. "Okay, Arpie, let's figure this out. Look, it's okay if you don't have a belly button."

Arpie raised his head and sighed again. "It is?"

"Sure. It doesn't make you less of a man... errr... robot. Just makes you special."

"I'm special?" Arpie took a step toward him. "You are the Jonas one, right?"

"Right. And this is Gordon." He waved his hand toward Gordon. "We helped build you. Gordon here, he's the software man, and I'm the hardware."

"Hardware. That is what I am. Just a pile of metal. A pile of hardware. A pile of junk." Arpie sighed. "You can't think if you aren't alive and you can't be alive if you don't have a belly button. The only logical conclusion is, if I don't have a belly button and I don't have a mother, I'm an orphan. An orphan pile of junk that can't think." He put his huge hands up to cover his face and slumped. "Nobody wants me."

"Ahh, come on, Arpie," Gordon said. "That's not true. We want you, and the wicked wit--errr--Doctor Habershaw wants you. She came up with the idea for you, you know."

"She did? You want me?" He spread his fingers and peeked between them. "Why?"

Jonas ran his hand through his hair. "Why, what?"

"Why do you want me? I'm flawed. You said so yourself."

"Well, because you're unique. Because you are one of a kind. Because…"

"Look, Arpie," Gordon cut in. "You are not

flawed. You just need a little tune up. That's all. We all need a little help occasionally."

"Then why did you say I had a flaw?" His eyes flashed brightly as he moved his hands from his face and pointed at Gordon. "Don't deny it. I heard you say it." Arpie sank to the floor and contemplated where his belly button would be if he had one. "Woe is me, quoth the raven. Woe is me."

"What did he say?" Jonas looked at Gordon.

"Umm--I think he said, Woe is me, quoth the raven."

"That's what I thought he said." Jonas pointed his finger at Gordon's nose. "What did you program him with?"

"Nothing--I just thought a little culture wouldn't hurt. You know a little Shakespeare, a little Poe, a little…"

Arpie started humming softly, then with a metallic harmony that was only barely reminiscent of the old tune, *Oklahoma*, he began to sing, "Oh, if I could only think, I think that I would think of cabbages and kings. If I could only think, I think that I would think of jelly muffins and belly buttons."

Jonas stared at the robot. "He's…"

"Singing," Gordon finished for him. He grinned. "Well sort of singing. I guess we didn't give him much in the harmony department, or the rhyming department either." He chuckled.

Jonas whirled and shook a menacing finger in Gordon's face. "What is so funny? We've got a disaster here, and it's all your fault."

"My fault?" Gordon backed away from the flaying digit. "How is it my fault? And watch the finger. I could lose an eye the way you're waving that thing around."

"You'll lose a lot more than an eye if we don't fix this." Jonas turned back to Arpie who had stopped singing and was once again staring at his mid-section. "Oh, woe is useless me," he sighed.

"You can think, Arpie. Now stop being such a wuss!" Gordon said.

Arpie looked at Gordon and back at Jonas. "You are nicer than him," he said.

Jonas almost smiled, but not quite. "Yep, and smarter too."

"Yes, I suppose you are, but how would I know? I can't think so I must take your word for it. Since you are so smart, you must know I'm useless. Just dismantle me and throw my bones into the junk pile."

"You don't have any bones," Jonas reminded him.

"True. Just plastic and metal parts. Well, toss my parts anywhere. Maybe you can build a nice coffee table with them. At least I'd be useful that way." Arpie sighed again and stood silent, his eyes flashing a solemn yellow.

Jonas ran his fingers through his hair and turned from the sulking robot to look at Gordon. "Okay, that's enough. We've got to do something before Habershaw sees this. Come on, we have to talk." He grabbed Gordon's arm and tugged him toward the door. "Arpie, you wait here. We'll be right back."

"Sure, I will stay here. What else can a useless pile of junk do? I am completely and utterly lost."

"Oh, for..." Gordon started.

"Shut up, Gordon," Jonas said and pushed him through the door. "Okay, here's what we're going to do," he said, shutting the door behind him. "We're going to use a little psychology here."

"Psychology?" Gordon asked. "On a robot? What kind of psychology would that be? Hey, we could call it Robology. Yeah, we'll be famous. The Robology experts. Hey, we could get rich."

Jonas sighed. "Would you just shut up and listen, you idiot! We're going to give him a belly button."

"Huh?" Gordon scratched his chin. "What good would that do? And how do you give a hunk of metal a belly button?"

Jonas smiled. "Easy. A few minutes with a cobalt drill will give Arpie a shiny, new belly button."

"I don't know," Gordon said, shaking his head.

Jonas reached for the drill. "Come on, what could go wrong?"

An hour later, Arpie stuck his finger in his new belly button. "Is this really my belly button?"

Gordon smiled and pulled his shirt up to show his belly button. "Sure. Look. It's just like mine."

"Wow, now I can think," Arpie said. Suddenly, he assumed the position of the *Rodin's Thinker* and refused to move. "Leave me alone," he said. "I'm thinking."

Six months later in the laboratory on the coldest moon Doctor Habershaw could find, Arpie was still sitting and still thinking.

Gordon and Jonas discussed him over a game of checkers. "Can't dismantle him 'cause he's too expensive," Jonas growled.

At least he's low maintenance. No food. No energy. Just takes up space," Gordon said, glancing at the thinking Arpie and moving a checker. "King me."

* * *

BIO: S. Joan Popek was owner and editor of Millennium Science Fiction & Fantasy Magazine and The Roswell Literary Review. She also wrote a monthly column called Ask Dr. WEB-Write for Millennium. She has been published in over 250 fiction, nonfiction and poetry works in various magazines. Her books, The Administrator, Sound the Ram's Horn, and Fairy Tales with a Freudian Flair are available from Amazon. The Administrator won the 2000 EPPIE Award, and her nonfiction book, Jumpstart Your Career with Electronic Publishing, was a 2002 EPPIE Finalist.

http://www.sjoanpopek.com/

Mount Bad Luck
by L. Edward Carroll
Contest Judge & CWI Staff

Samuel and Matthew Bigalow, retired 65-year-old twin bachelors, lived in an unassertive home in a shy village that some might call Dullsville, USA. Samuel, the oldest by two minutes, looked up from the Weekly Reporter and said, "Matt, why don't we do something out of the ordinary? Let's take a road trip."

Matthew's eyes never left the crossword puzzle. "Whatever for?"

"We aren't getting any younger and we should do it while we can. We've never even seen what the rest of the country looks like."

"Humph," Matthew grunted. "It's pretty much the same wherever you go. Don't see any reason to go traipsing around the countryside."

Samuel sighed and turned the one-page Weekly Reporter to the flip side.

Matthew removed his reading glasses and laid them on the book of crosswords. "Where, pray tell, would we go?"

"Don't know for sure."

"Well, wherever it is, I'm not coming, so count me out," Matthew said.

"Fine, I'll go by myself. Don't want the company of an old grump anyway."

"And how do you plan on going? We only have one car and I need it."

"I need it, too. Or do you want me to take a cab, or maybe ride a bike?"

"Either one is fine," Matthew said.

Samuel looked from his paper. "That isn't going to happen, brother. All you have to do is go with me and the problem is solved."

Matthew re-hooked his reading glasses behind his ears, and went back to his crossword. "Ain't gonna happen, brother," he said.

Samuel shrugged, scooted his chair to the kitchen table, and went back to reading the local rag. Well, not really reading. More like conniving how he could convince his stay-at-home brother to join him on an adventure to West Virginia. He had no idea why this sudden urge pressed him day and night. He looked at his brother sitting in his La-Z-Boy, laboring over the crossword puzzle. The two had never ventured more than 40 miles outside their village, but now the Alleghany Mountains beckoned.

Early the next morning, Samuel sat in the blue Ford Explorer honking the horn.

Eventually, Matthew, sleepy-eyed, sparse hair looking like a long-abandoned bird's nest, cracked the front door to see what the racket was about.

Samuel stuck his head out the car window. "Hurry up and get dressed. I'm leaving with or without you. By the way, your stuff is already in the car. Bring your crossword books."

Matthew shouted back. "Hold your horses, you old fool. I gotta bring my cup of coffee," and he disappeared, grumbling.

Once on their way, Samuel tried to assure Matthew, as well as himself. "You're going to enjoy this. We're off to West Virginia and the Allegheny Mountains. I've always wanted to see how the people live up there."

"Humph. Like I said… it's all the same wherever you go, Sam."

"It's a very different world out there and we need to check it out."

Matthew remained unimpressed, slumped in his seat, staring at boring cornfields. After a day and night of driving, the Alleghenies made their appearance in the distance.

"You call those mountains?" Matt sneered. "They're just big, gray hills."

"Wait 'til we get closer. You'll see."

"And how would you know? Neither of us has been more'n fifty miles from Alma, Michigan. It's a waste of time and money. Besides, I'm hungry and tired and I have to pee. We haven't seen a gas station or an exit for the last three hours. Some trip this is."

Sam pulled over to the side of road.

"What are we stopping for? Something wrong?" Matt said.

"You said you gotta pee. Have at it."

"Are you crazy?"

"No. Just get out and let 'er rip."

"And if a cop comes?" Matt said.

"I'll just tell him we have a hot wheel and you're cooling it off."

"A hot wheel? Are you serious?"

Sam grinned. "Sure. Just cool that front tire down and have fun doing it."

"I think you've got a screw loose! Hot wheel, indeed. Never heard such nonsense," Matt muttered as he opened the door.

The trip continued without incident. The old Ford Explorer climbed the mountains without a sputter, and interesting sights began to appear.

Sam pointed to a log cabin off to the right. "Now, look at that, Matt. That's a *real* log cabin. Not one of those store-bought jobs."

"Humph. You're right… for a change."

They rode in silence for a time, and Sam took sudden interest in a farmer walking behind a team of two huge mules, their dark hides shining with sweat, slowly plowing black earth on an impossibly steep hillside.

"How in the world…" Matthew started to ask.

"I told you, it's a different world out here. If that guy tried to plow with a tractor, it would tumble down the hill."

"Humph. That's the second time you've been right, but don't get cocky about it," Matt said.

The road steepened, twisted with hairpin turns and climbed at right angles all the way to the top where stomach-dropping cliffs dived to sea level. The vertical sides of the mountains rose in a fusion of granite slabs, gnarled tree roots, and hovering moss-covered rocks that waited for the slightest tremor to set them free.

Samuel opened the windows to breathe in the heady, pine-scented air, then shifted to a lower gear and pumped the brakes to slow their descent.

"What if one of those big rocks fall?" Matt said, looking up.

"Well, that wouldn't be a good thing, would it? But they've been up there forever, so don't worry about it. Look down there," Sam said, pointing to a valley. "Isn't it beautiful?"

"Humph! We're about to die, and you want to sight-see. We can look at it later, *if* one of those stupid passing trucks doesn't push us off this stupid cliff before a stupid boulder smashes us to dust."

Sam just laughed, and passed a heavily graveled road that ended quite suddenly at a sand pit.

Matthew stared at it. "Why in the world did they build a road to nowhere?" Before Samuel could answer, Matthew shivered as it dawned on him... *a catch ramp for runaway vehicles.* "Never mind, I know."

Twenty minutes later, the twins spied a tiny village in the valley. It reminded Samuel of a model railroad set he had a long time ago.

Samuel spoke first. "Just look at that. It's like a picture postcard."

"That's the third time you've been right today. It's downright scary," Matt said.

"How strange. Two identical churches facing one another. I'll bet there's a history behind that," Samuel said.

"Indeed, and notice how every single building is the same exact shade of brilliant white. Looks like they painted the whole town yesterday," Matt said.

Samuel pulled over and the twins took pictures of the strange little village with their phones. "Why do you suppose they'd want two churches in such a small village? Let's take a closer look," Sam said.

"Suit yourself. Maybe they have a restaurant. I'm starved."

They drove down deserted streets, straining for the sight of a single person. "Isn't this Saturday?" Sam said. "And not a single shop is open for business? It's as silent as a tomb. Look at that. A drug store, grocery store, a feed and hardware store, a hotel and restaurant, all closed. Even the gas station. Yet every store's window is full of antiques. Where is everybody?" Sam said.

"Maybe it's some kind of mountain holiday," Matt said, yawning.

"Uh-uh. Something isn't right. I don't like it. Let's check out the churches."

The steeples, front doors, founding date, stained glass windows, steps, and sidewalks were mirror images. Both signs read, *First Baptist Church.*

"I don't feel good about this, Sam. Too weird. I'm getting really bad vibes. Where are the cars? Pets? Kids? Let's get out of here."

"Just a minute," Sam said, opening his car door. He expected the smell of fresh paint. Instead, he inhaled the vile, pungent odor of burnt wood and ashes… and charred human flesh. Half in and half out of the car, he froze, sniffed again, got back in and shut the door.

"What?" Matt said.

"Nothing. Just, just… nothing." Samuel started the car, trying to calm his nerves.

"You don't look so good," Matt said. "Your hands are shaking."

Samuel held one hand out. Sure 'nuff. "When I started to get out, I got the most awful feeling, and I smelled fire and brimstone." He looked at Matt, expecting ridicule. "I swear I could."

"Well, that's a heck of a thing," Matt said. "Everything looks as fresh as a daisy. I'm going into the church."

"No, Matt! Don't go. For the life of me, I can't understand it, but I can't stop shaking."

Matt paused. "Okay. Let's go."

Samuel proceeded down the main street until they approached a railroad crossing sign. "I don't remember crossing a set of tracks, do y…"

With no warning whatsoever, a speeding train sliced through like a hurricane, clattering, roaring, smoke stack belching black smoke. No warning signals. No horn.

Samuel slammed on the brakes, staring back at the passengers who stared at them, but before anyone could speak, the train and the tracks disappeared.

The twins looked at each other. Through chattering teeth, Matthew said, "D-did you s-s-see th-that?" The color drained from his cheeks and he visibly aged before Sam's eyes.

"We're okay. We're okay," Sam said, patting

Matt on the knee. Sam took a few deep breaths, calmed himself, and they proceeded down the mountain with great care. Neither felt inclined to speak for some time.

At the foot of the mountain, an *Open* sign flashed in a window.

"We'd better stock up on snacks and drinks," Sam said. "Maybe they'll have sandwiches, too."

Matt nodded, still unwilling to speak.

The old lady at the counter didn't own a smile. Her shifty eyes followed the twins through the store as though they were about to don clown masks and rob her at gunpoint. When they approached the counter with their purchases, she rang them up. "Anything else?" she finally said as she subtotaled.

"Yes, ma'am," Samuel said. "We found a beautiful but deserted village in the mountains. Where is everybody? There's not a living soul in it... except for the train that passed through."

"Train? Village? There ain't nothin' on Mount Bad Luck. Nothin' at all. I don't know what you're talkin' about."

The brothers looked at each other, then at the old woman. "Sure, there is," Samuel said. "We both saw it. The whole town's been freshly painted in glistening white. There are two mirror image churches, identical in every way. Even with the same name, and they face one another. Strange thing is, nobody's there. No people. No cars. No animals. The stores are fully stocked with antiques, but no one is there."

"I don't know what y'all been smokin' but I'd like to have some. There ain't no town up there. I oughta know. I drive over it every day to work and back."

"But I've got pictures of it," Samuel said. "Look at these." He pulled his phone out and scrolled through the pictures, but pictures of seared rubble replaced those of the enticing village. No stores. No houses. No churches. The brothers stared at the phone, awestruck.

Both men missed the pure evil gleam that escaped the old woman's eyes.

Matt's mouth dropped open. "But we saw it. We took pictures. And a passenger train barely missed us. There was no warning at all. It was like it appeared out of thin air. The tracks weren't there one minute and the next they were, and then they disap..."

Samuel tapped his arm and gave the high sign to zip his lip. They pocketed their phones, scooped up their snacks, and headed for the door.

"Hold it!" the woman said.

They turned.

"That'll be $25.69."

Sam nodded to Matt, who paid the bill, and the two men left the store abruptly, glad to be gone.

The old woman stood on the porch and watched them disappear into the distance. "Roger!" she yelled. "Get out here."

Roger appeared in a puff of smoke. "Yes, ma'am?" he said.

"Did you hear that?"

"Yes, ma'am. Why'd you let them go?"

"So's they'll tell everybody they meet about our village."

"I don't think that's a good idea."

"Did I ask you? I'm the High Priestess, and I'll do as I see fit."

"Yes'm, but that was seventy-years ago, before the big fire. Never seen nothin' like it. That ole lightnin' lit up the sky and struck the churches and the mountain and the whole world turned red." Roger stood with stringy black hair and slumped shoulders, shaking his head. "Folks say the engineer must'a been sound asleep 'cause the train plunged right into it without so much as hittin' a brake," he said.

"I know. The twin covens went up in smoke, too. We were lucky to escape. And those two gents saw the train! Very few have, so I think there's something special about them."

"Maybe so. But respectfully, what if they blab about the village to everyone they meet?"

"You still don't understand, do you, dummy?"

"No, ma'am. I reckon not." He looked down.

"I *want* them to tell everyone they meet."

"Why? Somebody might believe 'em, ma'am."

"No, they won't. They'll come see for themselves, and we'll repopulate Mount Bad Luck with them. We've had to wait seventy-five Hallows' Eves. The timing is perfect."

"Yes, ma'am. It is."

Meanwhile, Samuel pushed the Explorer a few clicks over the speed limit. "Matt, I think I've had enough travelling. What say we go home?"

Handing a cold, frosted bottle of Orange Cream soda to Samuel, Matt said, "That's a splendid idea. We have an earful to tell the Bridge Club about Mount Bad Luck."

"*And* everyone else we meet," Sam said.

* * *

BIO: L. Edward Carroll is a graduate of Long Ridge Writers Group, The Institute of Children's Literature, and is a former writing tutor at A-1 Writing Academy. He also has a background as a Computer Systems Analyst, has an Economics major, and is a former entrepreneur. Born and raised in Greenfield, Massachusetts, this ex-Marine drill sergeant now devotes himself to drilling fledgling writers at Creative Writing Institute.

The Destination
by Emily-Jane Hills Orford
Contest Judge and CWI Staff

"I am completely and utterly lost," I said aloud to myself. Sitting in the cold, dark car, somewhere in the middle of nowhere, I was really starting to question my sanity. To be out driving at night was not something I enjoyed at the best of times. But in the country? Without streetlights to mark the path? And with critters of all description dashing across the road barely within the stretch of my high beams? Not my finest moments. Muttering to myself was calming. What I should be doing was screaming.

I was lost. My GPS was useless on these country roads, and without an address, there was no point in trying to coordinate the device. Written instructions were on the passenger seat, within reach. But it was dark. And whenever I turned on the cabin lights, I couldn't see well. It didn't matter. I had the instructions memorized. At least, I thought I did.

Aunt Vera had insisted I come. Immediately. She didn't say why. And she didn't say where. Not really. My aunt was very cryptic at the best of times. Her directions were downright bizarre.

Aunt Vera lived in a small house in the country.

"Don't come to my house," she said in a raspy voice that barely carried across the cell channels.

Much to my mother's dismay, she was pretty self-sufficient. Mother, Aunt Vera's younger sister, lived in a slick condo in downtown Toronto. A lawyer by trade. I had no idea where my father was. Or who he was for that matter.

I was like Mother. To a point. I was a lawyer, too. I worked at the same law firm. I lived in Toronto, but in a house, not a condo, and I had a small garden I loved to putter in. Mother was forever telling me to wash the dirt from under my nails. There was also a bit of my aunt in me, much to Mother's chagrin.

"I'm not at home, you know. You won't find me at my house," Aunt Vera had said. Her country cabin was a good three-hour drive from downtown Toronto, two hours being the time needed just to escape the city itself. Then it was a meandering drive north and east and then north again.

"Come as though you were going to my house, but carry on down my road." I could hear her voice in my head.

It was a typical country road--gravel, full of potholes, meandering, pitch black and all kinds of animals darted at random, unexpected intervals.

"Drive for about twenty minutes. There's another road. Turn right, then left, then right again.

Drive very slowly for another ten minutes. Flicker your headlights. Roll down your window and listen. I'll be hollering. Follow the sound."

Right.

Left.

Right.

Flicker lights.

Windows down.

No sound.

Unless you count coyote howls and crickets all around.

It was summer. It was warm. It didn't take long for the car to fill with hot, humid air and more mosquitoes than you'd want to see in a lifetime, let alone one night.

Still no hollering.

"Aunt Vera?" I took the initiative. No response. Even the coyotes fell silent. I pulled out my cell phone.

No signal.

Was it right, left, right?

Or left, right, left?

If I turned around would I be able to find my way back?

"Help!" Finally, a holler. It wasn't me, though I felt like hollering, but this call was just ahead and very faint.

I flickered the headlights again.

Another "Help!" A little louder this time. I was close. Still lost, but close.

I turned a bend in the road. My headlights picked up movement off to the side. I found a driveway and turned in.

"Aunt Vera?" I swallowed a mouthful of mosquitoes in the process. Ugh! One thing I hated about the country. Bugs!

"Over here," the voice said.

I put the car in park, but left it running, the high beams marking a clear path ahead. At least as far as the brush-thickened tree line. I reached into my handbag and pulled out the little flashlight I always carried. I flicked it on. It worked. Barely. I climbed out of my car and waved the light in a circular pattern, highlighting the darkness that enveloped the car's high beam projection. I walked forward, my shadow from the car's headlights stretching long and thin, casting darkness where my feet would soon tread.

I tripped.

Something my shadow had hidden.

A log?

A lump of something.

The flashlight tumbled from my hand and rolled out of reach as I fell to my knees. My headlights barely projected my position. As I crawled toward the fading beam of the flashlight, my hand touched another. It was very cold.

"Aunt Vera?" I grabbed the flashlight, now within reach, and used its dim beam to look more closely. The head twisted at an awkward angle, her face a ghastly white, and something dark smeared the front of a light-colored top. I felt for a pulse. There was none.

* * *

BIO: Emily-Jane Hills Orford, multi-award winning author of 21 books, has pursued her passion for writing stories about the 'real' people in her life. Her award-winning novel, *F-Stop: A Life in Pictures* (Baico 2011), is a story about her mother.

Her stories have appeared in History Magazine, Canadian Stories Magazine, and Western People, to name a few. After traditionally publishing several books, Emily-Jane turned to self-publishing. Ms. Orford is a true cross-genre writer that has written fiction and creative nonfiction short stories and novels for readers of every age.

http://emilyjanebooks.ca

The Awakening
by Mikel Wilson
Amazon Best Selling Author

He awoke in armor, groggy, and looked around. *Who am I? Where am I?* He rubbed his head. *I am completely and utterly lost.* He looked at his hands and body. Apparently, he was unharmed. He stood, dizzy, and staggered down the street to a tavern.

A cute waitress approached and savored his knight's armor. "Anything for you, hon?" she asked.

He shook his head.

"If you want anything, anything at all," she winked, "just let me know."

She sashayed across the room to serve another customer.

His ears detected a thumping from afar, and he turned to look. What was it? Didn't anyone else hear it? When he saw the waitress staring at him, smiling wide and winking again, somehow, he knew the thumping was the beating of her heart. This was not a good night for complications. He walked out.

A small sound in the night called to him, begged him to come. *Hurry!* He raced toward the calling, unsure of its location and followed the familiar smell to the edge of a woods. He walked the perimeter, homing in on the scent and the light footfalls.

A comely figure appeared in the shadows. When she spoke, it was like the medley of doves. "Robert?"

Was that his name?

They stared at one another and her silent tears turned into sobs. Long, flowing hair draped her shoulders, and now she was close enough for him to see the sparkle in her eyes.

A sparkle he remembered. But his head ached. "You know me? Who are you?"

The beautiful woman flew to his arms and hugged his neck. "How can this be? I thought you were dead. Where have you been?"

A flashback skimmed through his mind. He and the maiden were running in a beautiful field. Then they were in a castle where she was held prisoner. He could see himself toasting with a metal cup and sipping the poisoned wine. He heard her screams as he fell to the floor. "You escaped," he said. "How?"

"I stabbed the guard and crawled through a window. They're still searching for me. We can't stay here."

"But there is so much I want to ask," he said. "I don't remember much."

Her voice was colder, harder now. Seven years had changed her. Yes, he remembered a little. Her hair was longer now. She had strength and independence.

Was that part of the difference he felt? No. He almost staggered at the loss of warmth in her eyes.

"We don't have time for this," she said. "Don't you remember me?"

He nodded, tears welling in his eyes. One word crept from his mouth. "Alyssa."

She nodded her head. They embraced again and shared hungry kisses.

He questioned her as they walked hand in hand.

She stared at him often. "I still can't believe I found you," she said.

"What has happened in the past seven years? The last thing I remember was drinking the poison. And you were gone."

"I survived the best way I could," she said. "The sorcerer still seeks me. I can't quit running."

Robert waited for her to continue, but she didn't. The long walk ended at a cave. No wildlife. No vegetation. No grass. Nothing but a barren wasteland.

"Is this where you live?" he said.

"Yes. Come inside. I want you to meet someone."

As they entered the cave, light footsteps ran to meet Alyssa.

"Mother!" he cried out.

She squatted to hug him.

Robert noticed the birthmark on the boy's

shoulder--a birthmark identical to his. His knees quivered as truth dawned on his heart.

She took the boy by the hand and led him to Robert. "Jonathon, this is your father."

The child's eyes lit up. "Father!"

Robert knelt and opened his arms, then realized he sensed a strong presence that now entered the room.

Like a slow-motion movie, a whirlwind filled the cave.

Robert turned his head, hair flying in the breeze, and the demon sorcerer welled up out of the whirlwind's center.

Alyssa's eyes widened in panic and the boy's mouth opened to scream, but it was too late.

The demon held Jonathon by the neck and Alyssa by the arm.

"It would seem you survived, Robert," he said, as a dense fog formed at the floor of the cave and moved upward. "I'll deal with you later."

Alyssa's eyes screamed for help. "Robert! Find the gypsy. Find the gypsy!" And they were gone.

Robert drew his sword and dashed about like a madman, searching for his family. "No! No! No! Alyssa! Jonathon! I'll find you, if it takes the rest of my life." The knight fell to his knees and wept. "I swear it. I'll find you."

But how do you follow a vanishing apparition? Robert wandered for hours and found himself standing at the edge of murmuring water.

You are a hybrid, the water whispered in a beckoning call. *Smell. All of nature is at your command. Believe in yourself and follow your instincts.*

His feet seemed to know where to go, and he quit wrestling with things he didn't understand. An hour later, he stood at the edge of a river. His throat cried of thirst and his aching body yearned for a bath. He removed the heavy armor, and waded into the water, never suspecting the sneak attack of soft padding wolves. Roberts whirled at the sound of their footsteps.

The alpha male stood on the shore, his majestic form tall and strong, snarling. He and two others approached with lowered head and glinted eyes, waiting for the right opening. The alpha eyed Robert's sword on the shore and grinned. "Fear not, knight. We will make it quick."

Robert raised his eyes to the sky, and felt hidden strength emerging.

Suddenly, the alpha noticed the mark on his shoulder. "Stop! He is one of us." He transformed into a human that stood nearly seven feet high and weighed in at 400 pounds. He approached Robert with an outstretched hand, and when he walked, the ground quivered. "My apologies, brother," he said. "My name is Jason, and I am the leader of this pack. We mean you no harm."

Wolf-human hybrids. Robert spluttered, "Apology accepted," and shook the outstretched hand.

"Can we be of assistance?" Jason said.

"Perhaps. Do you know where the gypsy is? I need her help."

"She is deeper in the forest. She is an evil woman with vast knowledge and power. She may help you… or she may kill you for the fun of it."

"I'll take my chances," Robert said.

"I'll show you where she is, but after that you're on your own."

The pack walked many miles together until rays of the full moon struck Robert and his body began to change.

Jason and the pack also transformed, growled and bared their fangs.

Robert turned his back to them, but his body grew.

"What are you?" Jason said. "Turn and face me."

Robert's body rippled with muscles. His head rose to the moon and released a howl that could be heard for miles. Then he swung around to meet the pack with glowing yellow eyes and giant ears. His lips raised over razor-sharp teeth and spittle oozed out of his mouth. "I am a hybrid of two clans. One-part cheetah. One-part wolf." His form continued to swell.

Jason stepped back, and the entire pack bowed their heads in submission.

"I mean you no harm. I need help to find my wife and son," Robert said, fire leaping in his golden eyes.

Jason and the others backed away. "We leave you to your quest," Jason said. "Follow the creek and you will find the gypsy. If we can be of service, we will hear your howl and come at once."

"Thank you, my friends." The knight followed the stream. *Alyssa. Jonathon.* He fought the tears that begged to flow and made camp.

The morning sun crawled into the sky and breathed warm rays on a weary face. His eyes opened wide at the sight of a scampering rabbit. He dashed after it with breathtaking speed, caught it, and enjoyed the nutrition it provided.

Onward he walked, in search of the gypsy. Hours later, he discovered a peculiar pile of bones in an open field and a cave nearby.

This must be it. The knight approached with great caution, but nothing could have prepared him for the 30-foot alligator that waddled out of the cave.

Its mouth opened wide with a loud hiss and it ran straight for him.

Robert drew his sword, sprang over the beast and struck it in the side, but the gator's tail slammed him into a tree. The knight shook his head and gathered his wits for the coming onslaught.

The monster approached more warily, hissing, eyes glowing, and with every step, his body grew.

Robert's eyes bulged at the sight. He swallowed hard. A bit of caution might be in order. The beast attacked again, and Robert attempted to keep the tree between them.

The alligator lifted its head high and roared, and then gnawed on the tree and surrounding limbs to catch the mighty knight.

Robert sidestepped and dodged. On the next lunge, he struck the beast's side with all his might.

The huge gator rolled onto its side, and clawed its way back to its feet. Furious and blind with rage, the beast's color changed to crimson red.

The knight dodged behind one tree and then another, but nothing could stop the monster now.

It plowed through trees or broke them in half with mighty jaws.

Robert backed into an outcropping of rocks and found himself short on time and space. He flattened himself against a boulder and held the sword up like a tiny toothpick.

Fortunately, the overgrown lizard wanted to play with his quarry before eating him. The long red tongue flicked over Robert, inhaling the knight's odor, tasting his sweat, tantalizing its own appetite. When Robert made a mad dash, the gator grabbed him by the leg, lifted him into the air and shook him.

Drooping from the gator's mouth, helpless and in agony, Robert fought the blackness that pulled him down. The gator was taking him into the swamp. If Robert didn't make his move now, it would be too late.

Alyssa and Jonathon need me.

With one last mighty effort, Robert stabbed his sword in the gator's snout and pushed it in all the way to the hilt.

The alligator's color instantly changed from crimson to green, lifted its head for a shrill scream that shook the earth, and dropped its prey.

Blood spewed from Robert's leg like a fountain as he watched the creature retreat, swinging its head wildly, banging against trees and rocks. He raised his battle-worn body, and peered at the gypsy that now approached.

Tattered clothes hung from a withered body that slumped with age, and her voice trembled when she said, "You came a long way to die." She twisted a finger and an unseen force slammed her prey against a rock wall.

Robert hung in mid-air, scarcely able to breathe, shouting, "Let me go!" in a squeaky voice.

"*You* are commanding *me*? So, so funny, when you can't even get down. You come to my home, attack my pet, and command me to serve you? Humph. You're a waste of what little time I have left." The gypsy lifted an arm and began chanting.

"Nooo!" Robert yelled. "Please. I came to ask your help, and I didn't know that thing is your pet. It attacked me. I was only defending myself. Please, I need your help. At least hear me out."

"You need my help for what?" She asked with a curious grin. "To right all that is wrong? To restore the kingdom? To stop the evil? Hmm? Bah. There will always be evil." She flipped her hand over and the knight fell to the ground with a hearty thump.

Robert struggled to his feet, and attempted to walk on his mangled leg, but loss of blood and agonizing pain won the battle and he fell into blackness.

The old gypsy gazed at his unconscious body and walked around him, smiling. She held one hand over him, levitated his body, and moved him into the cave without effort. "I must be older than I thought. I had almost forgotten the pleasure of seeing a handsome young man." The gypsy removed his armor and rubbed a wrinkled hand across his hairy chest. "Ah, this one is special," she said. "I will hear what he has to say."

When the knight awoke, his wounds were bandaged, his pain eased, and his mind at rest.

"So, you're finally awake," she said with a cackle. "Good. You look like you've been missing too many meals lately. I have some stew for you. My name is Kelsy. Now who are you and what do you want?"

Weeks passed, and Kelsy trained him relentlessly, day and night. "You can do better, young knight. Be faster. Stronger. Braver. If you aren't, that demon will make a rug out of your pasty white skin."

Finally, well-equipped, in good health, and well-trained, the hybrid knight set out to rescue his family. In two weeks' time, Robert found the castle which was covered in perpetual darkness.

Evil smothered the air.

The knight groped through the pitch-black, running his hands around the castle until he felt two large doors. He backed up and hit them with all his might. After several attempts and a sore shoulder, the doors caved.

Much to his surprise, a small, warm glow followed him inside, as though a little goodness was invading a nest of pure evil. "I am here to claim my family," he shouted.

A dark, sinister laugh filled the castle. "You are here to claim your death," the voice said. A silver body suddenly appeared on the throne, as though the being were made of pure armor, but even scarier were the eyes... eyes that were nothing but black holes with no irises or pupils.

Robert felt like he would fall into the pit of hell itself if he stared at those eye sockets too long.

The thing raised one hand and an army of the living dead appeared in the form of deformed minions. Short, ugly little things that could change their appearance and weapons at will. "So, you want your family! Very well. They can watch you die." The sorcerer snapped his fingers and Alyssa and Jonathon appeared at his side.

"Robert, you came!" Alyssa said.

"I told you I would," Robert said. He lifted his head and loosed a howl that chilled even the demon.

Immediately, slinking wolves entered the chamber, snarling, surrounding the army of minions. Slobbering. Drooling for fresh blood. Ears laid back. Lips curled high above their fangs. Measuring their foe. Squatting their haunches to spring.

Jonathon transformed to a wolf and joined the rest of the clan.

Robert transformed also as he led the charge for the war of control over the realm.

Sharp teeth struck metal. The minions screamed and pulled back, stabbing the wolves with lances and swords, but the wolves' bodies healed instantly unless they received a mortal blow to the head. Green eyes squinted to a sliver as they charged repeatedly, slashing, biting, and grabbing their prey by the throat.

The demon raised his hand again and a second swarm of minions appeared.

Just when the wolves seemed to be outnumbered and all hope was lost, Kelsy appeared in the midst of the melee. When the demons prevailed, the room had scarcely any light, but when the wolves, Robert and Kelsy prevailed, the room grew brighter.

Several wolves lay mortally wounded, and their bodies changed back to humans when they died.

Kelsy used her powers to make the minions disappear, or slashed them with a flying sword, but when a lucky minion stabbed her in the back, she collapsed with a screech. She could save others, but she could not save herself.

Robert fought his way to her side and gently lifted her head.

"There is no time, my young friend," she said. "Prepare to battle with everything that is in you." Kelsy raised her hand and nearby minions turned to ashes that fell in tiny heaps on the floor. *"Now, Robert! Attack the demon, now!"*

"I'll be back," he said, and then fought his way to the sorcerer with renewed strength that would not be denied. "Sorcerer, your time for judgment has come."

The demon laughed as he sidestepped Robert's blow, caught him off guard and struck him hard.

Again and again, Robert attacked, and the sorcerer buffeted him.

Kelsy watched from afar, filled with rage and indignation. "Alas, the demon is too strong for my knight." She raised a trembling arm and pointed at the demon.

Oh, stones, awake, and castle shake
Armor fall, and most of all, Demon... be gone!

The castle walls began to quiver and quake as the battle ensued. The floor split and minions fell through the widening cracks. Robert's armor was gone because of the chant, but so was the demon's. The room grew brighter and brighter as might met right.

Robert's renewed energy gave him strength for one more attack, and this time, his sword met flesh.

The sorcerer grabbed his wounded arm and knocked Robert aside, then marched over to Kelsy and spit on her. "You meddling, old hag. You seem to like this lad. Now watch me kill him. By the way, before you die, know this--I am the one who killed your mother when she refused to be my queen."

Kelsy wheezed and spoke with great effort. "You... will die here."

"I think not," he said, and when he walked toward Robert, the room grew darker. The demon stretched his hand toward Robert and pushed him against a wall. The sorcerer beckoned a sword that flew through the air and buried itself in the knight's stomach.

Alyssa screamed.

Blood dripped from Robert's mouth, and his eyes bulged in pain. But that wasn't enough. The demon stepped closer and held out his hand, and then curled it into a fist that snapped Robert's ribs. The brave knight shrieked in pain and slumped.

The sorcerer laughed and approached for the final blow, but a young wolf named Jonathon leapt onto his back and fastened his jaws around the back of his neck.

Kelsy watched from afar and lifted a trembling arm to strike one more blow. A bolt of lightning sizzled as it pierced the sorcerer and the throne room brightened. For the space of thirty seconds, Kelsy and the sorcerer traded blasts of bolts, power bursts, and liquid fire. The room lightened, then darkened, then lightened again, and when Kelsy's body grew pale, struggling for breath, the demon loosed laughter that shook the foundations.

With furrowed brow, black eyes, and black nails an inch long and growing, his mouth twisted into a snarl and yellowed teeth turned black as the fullness of evil filled his body. When his eyes glowed red, the gypsy gave up, but with no warning whatsoever, the demon's mouth opened wide, his eyes turned silver, and his head parted from his body. Black blood sloshed over the floor, and his head rolled across the brilliant room.

And there stood Alyssa, holding a bloody sword in her hand and staring at the disembodied head. She ran to the old gypsy, and knelt by her side. "I don't know you, m'lady, but I thank you for helping my mate. Do him but one more favor as he stands dying at this moment. Oh, please, save him. I know you can."

A tear came to Kelsy's eye. "Quick-ly… p-put my br-bracelet on… h-his arm. Hur – ry."

Alyssa kissed her cheek, ripped off the bracelet, ran to Robert and put it on his wrist.

Nothing happened.

His cheeks paled.

Breathing stopped.

His body crumpled.

Alyssa struggled to support his weight, crying, and calling for Jonathon. She and the boy laid Robert on the floor and pulled the sword out of him.

"I'm too late. Robert! Come back to me. Please don't leave me." With tears dripping from her cheeks and onto his faced, she pressed her lips to his, pushed his hair back and wept. "I will love you forever."

Robert's eyes fluttered and Alyssa gasped.

"Do you mean that?" he said in a weak tone.

But her joy was short-lived when she thought of the old woman. "Robert, your friend is very near death."

With ever increasing strength, the young knight rose and stumbled to Kelsy's side. The old gypsy's eyes smiled.

"My sweet friend, Robert, you have defeated the tyrant and saved your family. What will you do next?"

"I will rebuild this kingdom, and I will name this castle Kelsy Hall," he said.

Kelsy smiled, gasped, and closed her eyes for the last time.

As Robert bent to kiss her, her body disappeared. He stood, "Goodbye, my friend." The knight turned to Alyssa and Jonathon, holding each by the hand, and the three mounted the steps to his new throne. Sunbeams burst through the windows and frolicked in the air while wolves slunk away and sang to the sky.

* * *

BIO: Mikel Wilson is an author from Sweetwater, Alabama. He is the father of four and married to his best friend, Danielle Wilson. His novella, *A Light Beyond the Darkness*, and Book 1 to The Hybrid Series, was number one on Amazon in three categories for ten days.

Christmas Letter
by Robin Currie
Bestselling Author

I could not bring myself to write it. How could I commit the events of this year to one single spaced page with a clipart reindeer in the corner? How could I share everything that happened when I could make no sense of it myself?

In hopes of finding the right words, I looked through the mail that had already arrived from overachiever friends who got their cards and letters out well before Christmas.

Some letters jumped off the page and shouted yippee!

"Lea earned a great deal of playing time for the Chargers soccer team."

"Stephen's Eagle Scout ceremony was in January, and he had a lead part of Buffalo Bill in the high school play."

I smiled. There had been years like that for us-- the pages filled easily with school honors and graduations and recitals, when each step of child rearing had been filled with delight I could not wait to share.

Some letters I read must have been harder to

write, but they seemed to have adjusted to the events.

"As this year comes to a close, our family is happy to see it go."

"Fred has made the big decision to retire. The company was bought out. I will be the breadwinner."

Other letters were just full of the change of living.

"The hot tub was moved out of the garage and on the deck outside our bedroom."

"We'll miss the newlyweds this year as they visit the 'in-laws' in California."

I sighed. Was there a time when change was exciting? Before now, I had made change sound like an adventure.

A few letters were unusual in the lack of the unusual.

"Our parents are in pretty good health considering their ages."

"Earl and Walter are still farming, although there are complaints about grain prices."

I wondered how all the *normal* years slipped by. How could I have forgotten to give thanks for those years when *nothing much* happened?

As I continued to read letters, I counted five weddings or engagements, six funerals, seven job changes or losses, three new grandchildren, two recoveries from major illness and three significant accidents in their letters. And twenty-two vacations. My friends did a lot of living this year.

Like sitcoms that wrap everything up in thirty minutes, all these letters ended upbeat.

"Our faith is still intact."

"We can withstand anything."

Nowhere did I find anything that was not neat and tidy, nothing messy and out of control, as this year had been for my best friend.

Now she was gone.

There would be no more Christmas letters from her. *I am completely and utterly lost*, I thought.

Suddenly, something niggled at me. Snatching my address book, I confirmed my suspicion.

A close friend who always sent long letters about her children's accomplishments, her spouse's success, and vacations in Vail, had not written this year. The silence was deafening. Had the wonderful children flunked out of school? Had the spouse been hauled in by the IRS for tax evasion? Surgery? Divorce? Miscarriage? House fire? Too busy?

The least they could do was say so!

I would not stop being a friend or stop caring. Could their lives be as confused and complicated as mine?

The least I could do was say so!

I took out a piece of paper and began to write.

"Dear friends, I hardly know where to begin. I have often felt lost this year, numbly doing what had to be done. If someone had told me last January what my situation would be now, I would have asked for a year's hibernation. I am relying on you, my friends, to understand. It all began last March…"

The writing came faster now--some sentence fragments and wrong tense verbs. It was not an English assignment. It was an outpouring from my heart. No editing. Just photocopied and stuffed in envelopes.

I wondered how my friends would react. Would some find my words depressing? Would others cross me off next year's list? Would any of them respond and share their heart with me?

I had been honest. Perhaps that was the one lesson I learned this year. It was small comfort and offered little hope, but as I sealed the envelopes, I felt grateful for even that.

And there would always be next year…

* * *

BIO: Robin Currie grew up in downstate Illinois. She earned a Bachelor of Elementary Education from Western Illinois University and attained an MLS at The University of Iowa. Robin settled in Chicago where she edited preschool curriculum for David C Cook before working as

Youth Services department head at Palatine Public Library. Amazed in midlife to be called to ordained ministry, she attended seminary at LSTC for both M Div and D Min degrees. She served as Pastor at Grace Lutheran Church in Glen Ellyn until retiring. Now Robin does only what she loves: she reads to Headstart children weekly. Her books have sold over a million copies.

http://www.robincurrie.net/

The Ambassador
by Caroline Grace
Previous CWI Contest Winner

"Hey, you guys. Check this out." Keira spread the newspaper on the communal table in the coffee shop, carefully smoothing it with her hands.

"Seriously, Keira? Who reads the newspaper anymore?" Sadie scrolled through her newsfeed oblivious to Keira's scathing glare.

"Listen to this. It's in the personals column. *I am completely and utterly lost. Does this statement resonate with you on a basic instinctive level? We are looking for someone just like you. Get paid for sharing your story. Get paid even more if we choose you as an ambassador to lost people everywhere. Inquire at 320 N. Capitol, Suite A-5, Thursday, July 13, 2:00-5:00 p.m. only.*"

"Hey, I'm lost. Pay me." Sadie said.

"Me, too." Lanie said.

"Come on, you guys. Don't you think this is the least bit interesting?" Keira said. "I mean, I am completely and utterly lost all the time. And wouldn't it be cool to be an ambassador?"

Lanie looked skeptical. "That's so vague, though. Be careful. Make sure it's legit."

"Well, it's not like the interview's at someone's private house. It's downtown in the Capitol Building."

"That's kind of weird. Daniel went for an interview with them last week, but I think it had to do with breaking bad habits or stopping smoking or something," Lanie said between sips of coffee.

"Wait! What? Daniel smokes?"

"You're missing the point, Sadie. I'm saying he got paid for some gig he went to at the Capitol Building."

"Well, I'm going," Keira said. "I need the money. And it seems like Daniel survived okay. Plus, I wanna be an ambassador!"

Thursday arrived sultry and muggy, and Keira felt her long blond hair wilting as she walked into the Capitol Building. She paused only a moment in front of Suite A-5 before she strong-armed the heavy, windowless door and stepped inside. Even in the dingy light, she could see the room was full of people who did indeed look lost.

The chair behind the front counter was empty, but a handwritten poster instructed her to sign in on the tablet anchored to the counter. Keira complied and took a seat next to the only person in the room who appeared to be over 30.

An automated voice announced the next instructions over invisible speakers, "Nathan Barley,

Amanda Jude, and Crystal Andrews, please enter Door 2 and take a seat."

At that moment, three twenty-somethings emerged from Door 1 into the waiting area where Keira sat. She stared at the unremarkable people who made no eye contact and looked like the life had been sucked right out of them.

Nausea crept up in Keira's throat. Maybe this wasn't such a good idea.

By 8:00 p.m., Keira could hardly move. The interview hadn't been so bad, but she was exhausted. She flopped onto the sofa, legs tucked beneath her and sat holding the television remote, although the TV remained black. Truth be told, she wasn't interested in much of anything.

The phone rang. She stared at it, and finally moved to answer it.

"Hey, Lanie... no, I'm fine. I just forgot to call when I got home. It was kind of long and drawn out." (Pause) "No, I'm really okay. Just tired. Got paid $50 while I was there, and they said they liked me and asked me to consider being an ambassador. It's a long story, but I said I would so I got paid again. I have to carry this beeper thing and push the blue button if I have a question. I go back every week, or maybe twice a week, and every time I go, I get paid. Easy smeasy."

She waited for Lanie's answer, wishing the

conversation was over.

"The ambassador part will be kind of cool. I'm not allowed to discuss the details. Confidential. You understand. I'm just beat. See you tomorrow, okay?"

Sleep fell heavy and deep on Keira, bringing restless dreams she couldn't remember. She longed for the light of morning, but when it finally came, it held its own terror. She was due back at the Capitol Building today. For some reason, the thought made her stomach lurch.

She sprang from a laying position to sitting bolt upright in bed, and suddenly needed to move. Her feet scurried before they even hit the floor. She jumped into the shower before the water fully warmed, and emerged three minutes later with soap bubbles still on her arm. The four walls of the apartment seemed to move in with a crushing effort. Keira grabbed the first matching shirt and pants she found, and opted out of makeup entirely. Practically running past her nightstand, she grabbed her phone, car keys, and the black 3 X 3 transponder she received yesterday, throwing them into her purse on the run.

Once on the sidewalk, Keira paused and sucked in a deep breath. Cleansing. Reviving. But the restlessness continued. Like she was in a hurry to do something, but didn't know what. She dug through her purse in desperation and yanked her phone out. She punched #4 and it rang. Thank goodness he answered. "Daniel?"

"Yeah," he said. "You went, didn't you? I can tell."

"Meet me. I need…. I don't know what I need. But something."

"I know. I really can't stay very long, but I'm goin' to the mall if you wanna meet there. Maybe at the coffee shop?" he said.

"Exactly what I was thinking. Twenty minutes?"

Keira sped all the way, but as she neared the mall doors, her anxiety quieted. In the midst of the noise and madness of humanity, she finally felt peace. She belonged there. Suddenly, she felt his presence behind her. So clearly, so distinctly, that she didn't turn her head when she spoke. "Daniel."

"Yeah."

She rose, feeling his presence more than seeing it, and the two ordered coffee with the solemnity of one performing last rites. "What did we do? Do you remember?" Keira said, staring at the rising steam of java.

"Not really. I just know I leave with a bigger check every time I go, and then I go home and go to bed. Easy money!"

"Do you have a treatment today?"

"You know we can't talk about it," he said.

"Right, but--do you remember talking to a real human there? Or was it a video? Or maybe a robot?"

"If we talk about it, they'll know, Keira."

"We're at the mall, Daniel. Who's gonna hear us?"

"*Especially* at the mall. I can't afford to lose this job. I gotta go."

"Daniel, would you sit with me a minute? Just… keep me company?"

"I can't. Maybe later."

Keira watched him walk away. She pushed the blue button on her transponder, the one that responded when she had a question. A now-familiar tune, barely perceptible above the mall noise, played briefly and the black box was quiet again. She sat for a moment, trying to remember the question she wanted to ask. Oh, well.

That night, she called Daniel again. Why didn't he answer? He was the one person who might understand the crazy thoughts that flashed through her mind. Thoughts she could not pinpoint. Thoughts that left her muddled and confused.

Keira began to understand. Ambassadors were lonely people. They devoted a great deal of time to their training. But it wouldn't always be that way. In the meantime, she would tolerate the unwell people in her life. People who didn't even know they were unwell. People like her co-workers. Even her family. People who had no understanding of her urgent calling.

Keira pulled into the parking lot at the bank, vaguely aware she had taken two spaces. She took her time collecting her things and getting out of the car. When she finally clocked in, she was six minutes late.

"Hi, Keira! Late night last night? You look tired!" Lanie said.

"Just not sleeping well lately."

"I'm sorry. Hey, remember Holly that used to work here? She's meeting me and Sadie for lunch at 11:30. Wanna come?"

"Thanks, but I've got an appointment today."

"Well, if you change your mind… I'll tell her you said hi."

"But I didn't," Keira said under her breath. She glanced discreetly at her co-workers. *Not one of them is a real friend. They don't care anything about me unless I'm late for work or they need a fourth party for lunch. Whatever made me think we were friends? For that matter, whatever made me think I ever wanted this job?*

She had never questioned her friends or job before. She sat, head in hands, scratching the back of her neck. Keira reached for the phone and pulled up a picture of her parents, now three states away. Her finger lingered over the #2 key on her phone's keypad, but heard a voice in her head say, "Do not contact family members until your training is over. Just for a few days."

Instead of pushing Speed Dial 2, she pushed the blue transponder button and waited. The familiar music played. Calming. Soothing. Then she remembered something the trainers had prescribed. Scarlet-tipped fingers rummaged through her bag and emerged with an amber plastic pill bottle. These would help. She took two.

Days rolled into longer days and dreaded nights followed faster, one upon the next. Keira's bank account grew as her interest waned. TV held no interest and her oldest friends, presumably tired of rejection, seldom called any more. Daniel wouldn't talk to her, and the bank terminated her employment because she took too much time off for training. But it didn't matter. None of it mattered, really. The trainers at the Capitol Building would take care of her. Today's appointment had a different feel to it. An excitement stirred in the air and she couldn't wait.

The day had come!

"You are ready for service," a voice said.

She wondered later who said it.

"For now, go home and await further instructions. Be prepared for media coverage at 5 o'clock this afternoon."

I hope I'm ready. I want to be a good ambassador, Keira thought.

The trainer's enthusiasm was contagious, and Keira left energized. Walking back to the parking garage, she picked up her phone. Her finger hovered over the keypad, but the thought of an actual conversation seemed overwhelming. She opted for a text message instead.

"Lanie, I might be on TV at 5 tonight, on all the local channels. Tell Sophie. Daniel probably knows already. I'll DVR it." Why did she text her? Lanie wasn't her friend. She had no friends.

That old restless feeling returned, but she waited patiently for the text that arrived at 4:18 p.m.

Meeting is at the mall. Come now.

She quickly threw her equipment, transponder, and phone into her bag, grabbed her car keys, and jumped into her little blue car. Finally, some action. As she backed out of the garage, she looked up. She had left the front door standing wide open. It didn't matter. The trainers would take care of everything. No more worries. No more anxiety.

At exactly 5:00 p.m., with the front door still standing open and the house lights on, the television blared in a loop announcement, alternating with a 30-second warning tone:

The President has declared a national state of emergency. All citizens are urged to stay inside until further notice. At approximately 5:00 p.m. tonight, terrorists bombed every major mall in the United States with incendiary devices simultaneously delivered through thousands of suicide bombers. Early indications are that the suicide bombers were native-born US citizens in their twenties who answered personal ads in local newspapers across the country. Investigators believe they were screened, hand-picked, and hypnotized to respond in flash-mob style when triggered. The malls played a package of original music slated to air today at 5:00 p.m., the approximate time of the terror attacks, and it is believed the music may have been the trigger. Fatalities, injuries and other information are not yet available. Stay tuned for the President's address.

The monotone droning of the Emergency Broadcast System signal began to sound again on every television in the nation as Keira's DVR recorded the images of horror.

Keira achieved ambassador status, and she had, indeed, made national television.

* * *

BIO: Caroline Grace is a banker by day and a writer by night. In October, 2012, she was diagnosed with Parkinson's Disease. Writing is her therapy on bad days and her reward on good ones. She enjoys reading, gardening, cooking and creating recipes.

The Garden of Lost Memory
by Martha Readyoff
Previous CWI Contest Winner

"Will you help me look for it?" Leah pleaded. "It'll be fun, and you'll love the place."

"What is it exactly, this place?" Rachel asked, although both knew she didn't really need any persuading. She was curious about anything new.

"It used to be a farm, an estate actually… a grand old estate," Leah said, trying to sound a little affecting. "I used to go there when I was little, when it was a private estate. We had picnic drives there with horses and carriages." She often wanted to impress the cool and beautiful Rachel.

Rachel was not usually overwrought with awe. After all, she had been to Italy and had seen great art and old, lovely gardens by the score. She had been to Russia and had had lovers.

Leah had only been to Norway where she saw Munch's, *The Scream,* and to Mexico with her husband, Jim, but the Don Quixote Museum in Guanajuato could never compare with Italy's Colosseum or Il Duomo.

Jim… ah, Jim was such a blessing. Leah had never had lovers or boyfriends or admirers, but Jim was all hers. Sweet. Kind. Good. She was lucky to have him.

Arriving at the estate's winding drive ushered Leah into another time where present and past bled into one another in a disorienting chimera. The long sweeping lawns of rolling manicured grass bore the color of ripe limes. Leah's own lawn was brown and beaten. Jim mowed it regularly, relentlessly, and so it looked neat and kempt, but not prosperous, not luxurious.

Everything had an air of easy opulence at the estate. Statues of white marble peeked from the hedges lining the drive. They passed an Italian-styled gazebo on their right, a circular belvedere in which a peacock strutted in majestic monotony, unmoved by the grandeur around him. Here was no mere meretricious show of wealth, but real, old money from a capacious trust over many generations.

At the top of the driveway, Leah parked the VW Beetle before a view so comely the two women simply stared through the windshield, each coveting the vista.

"I remember this," Leah sighed with nostalgia, breaking their silent reverie.

"It's absolutely gorgeous," Rachel said.

They made their way across the empty parking area toward the garden entrance, white gravel crunching beneath their steps.

Leah was glad there were no other visitors. It felt like the old place had been waiting for her, as though her memories were shaping in the most startling detail, and this time she had a witness.

"So, remind me, what exactly are we looking for?" Rachel said in her softly cultivated voice.

Leah snapped her attention to the present. "A garden. A sunken garden, deep in the woods. It's at the end of a long carriage trail. I remember marble pillars and steps and a fountain. It was grown over when I first discovered it. The fountain was broken, but it was so magical, like something I had read in a book. I think a boy kissed me there, but now I'm not sure if it's a real memory or just something I imagined." Leah's brow furrowed slightly in contemplation as she tried to parse memory from imaginings. "Let's look around the gardens by the house first."

They met new loveliness at every turn--dewy dripping fountains and carefully scissored topiaries, aged statuary, effulgent beds of flowers and redolent herbs, terraces and pergolas and belvederes, a meandering stream bubbling with curious carp that kissed the lady's proffered fingers as they giggled. Birdsongs and the cat-calls of peacocks haunted the air.

When they came to a great wide fountain framed

in perfect symmetry with high hedges and rose beds, Leah said impishly, "It's like Heavenly Creatures."

Rachel smiled and they both laughed. For a moment, the idea of running in terrifying glee around the fountain flickered across their faces, but they no longer possessed the crazy energy of youth. Now in their early forties, today's silly impulses were tame pets sleeping at their feet.

For Leah, it was all a strange origami tapestry of past folding over present. The memories were undeniable, yet vague, like looking at her reflection in the midnight window above her desk. Clear, yet unclear. This was the place where her mind wandered after an evening of endless cocktail chatter in the house. This was where she imagined fireflies into fairies and chased them with cupped hands. This was where she plinked pebbles into the deep fountain and watched the water tremble in the moonlight.

"Hi, Leah?" a man called.

Leah turned to meet the voice. Freddie? She hadn't seen him in thirty years. Was he real? Where did Rachel go?

"Leah!" Freddie said, waving.

She held a hand up--the hand of a fifteen-year old. She felt the years fall away as the old blended with the new. Something made her think his mother had pressed him to approach her.

She was a nice lady who dressed elegantly and drove bright little hackney ponies. When she saw Leah she always said, "Freddie loves your hats." A most puzzling statement for a grown-up to make to a teenager about another teenager.

Leah didn't think much about it at the time as adults seemed bizarrely Martian anyway, but she wondered if Freddie liked her, and if his mother's comments were a secret cipher for arranging a betrothal.

Freddie walked across the little meadow from his mother's runabout to the shooting cart where Leah was hanging a bridle and wiping horse spit from the bit.

"Hi," Leah said, nervous and curiously expectant. He was cute, with those loopy blond curls, big eyes, and skin so white she could see a faint blue vein pulsing in his temple. He looked like a boy from a nursery rhyme, and not nearly as scary as most boys. She wanted to run to him and throw her arms around his neck. She knew what he was about to say, as though a play were being acted out.

"Why didn't you play your coach horn?" he asked.

Leah couldn't tell if it was an accusation or a flirt.

"*I* was playing," he went on, "so why didn't *you*

answer?"

"I did," Leah said in defense. "I just didn't play very much. I'm not very good. I can't play as well as you."

"Nobody plays very well. After all, it's just a coach horn. Who even plays it at all?" he said.

Leah wanted to continue, but this conversation was oddly confrontational and argumentative. Was this how boys and girls who kind of liked each other talked together? She was out of her depth. "I'm sorry," she said and meant it, wondering if she had missed in his tuneless toots and flatulent blasts some unrequited love song. Or a forsaken mating call. She had the distinct sense of loss, of a chance that slipped away. Suddenly she wanted to cry.

A weird chasm of time passed between them and it seemed to hold thousands of possibilities, like a spectacle of fireworks, but her brain locked her words and she watched the possibilities fizzle. Leah turned back to the bridle and continued to wipe foamy sweat.

Freddie shrugged and walked away.

The sense of loss welled in her and quiet tears fell, soaking into the warm, salty leather in her hands.

"Well, are you ready?" Rachel asked.

Leah turned to face her, mouth hanging open as she returned to the present.

Rachel's laugh illuminated her beautiful face.

"Well, do you want to find your secret garden, Mary Lennox?" she said.

"I, uh, have no idea where it is," Leah said, looking around. The last time she was here, she thought the garden fairies might be real, but her imagination always had a way of weaving itself through her thoughts, plaiting itself in league with reality. "Let's try over there," Leah said, looking for Freddie.

The women stepped lightly over the carpet of cushiony velvet toward the wilderness of the lost garden. Ghostly peacock calls floated up behind them.

At the edge of the lawn, they came upon the old carriage road. Close to civilization, it was wide and well kept, lined by white statues of Greek and Roman gods perched on high pedestals for better viewing. They walked along, looking at the statues and laughing at the name of the trail, *The Carriage Road of the Gods.*

"This one looks like Tony Curtis," Rachel said, laughing as she ran her finger along the stony sinew of Hercules' thigh.

Leah coveted Rachel's sensual movements, even her most banal gestures like paying a grocery clerk, moving a chair, opening a car door. All were a flirtatious ballet of her hands, eyes, legs, neck. Leah compared her own movements as oafish gestures that pushed people away, whereas Rachel's sang people to her like mute sirens. Her mind whirled as she imagined herself as a graceful ballerina.

"Me and Norma are going to explore. Want to come?" Freddie said.

Leah whirled around to see him approach with Norma, his older sister.

"Where did you go?" Leah said.

"Huh? What're you talking about? We've been here all afternoon."

Leah had finished cleaning the harness and watering Halifax and Hamilton, the pair of French Coach horses, and was about to find a quiet place to read *A Mid-Summer Night's Dream* for a book report. Something felt out of sequence. She looked about. Grown-ups burbled together, nibbling poached salmon, tomato aspic and caviar pies while sipping gin and tonics. Occasionally, a heady guffaw punctuated their quiet prattle.

"Okay," Leah said. She removed her bowler hat and asphyxiating cravat and placed them neatly in the boot of the carriage while Freddie and Norma waited. "Where do you want to explore?" Leah asked.

"Let's go this way." Freddie hurried down the narrow meadow, out-pacing Leah and his sister.

Norma chummily linked arms with Leah and listed her head toward her.

"Freddie likes your hats," she whispered, smiling, and then ran ahead. "Come on!" she called.

Leah trotted to catch up, wondering if she were the victim of a secret joke.

A lacework of shadows like kirigami ghosts closed over them all as they made their way further down the road, deeper into the woods, and could no longer hear the peacocks or see the outline of the house. Tufts of weeds sprang up first sporadically and then thicker and thicker, covering the road. The road narrowed to an artery and then a capillary, so much so that they all had to walk single file.

"This can't be right," Leah said. "I am completely and utterly lost. You can't drive a carriage through here." She looked up from the root-tangled path and could not see Freddie or Norma.

"Brrr, it's getting cold, Leah," Rachel said and endearingly rubbed Leah's goose-bumpy arms. "Want to head back?"

Where…? "What time is it? How long have we been walking?" Leah asked, searching pockets for her phone.

"I don't know," Rachel said. "I left my cell in the car, but it's starting to get dark." Rhododendron bushes were closing in on them like a blossomy womb.

"Yes, I think we should go back," Leah said. "I

think I forgot to leave a note. Jim might get worried."

"Okay," Rachel said. "We wouldn't want to worry Jim."

At the mention of Jim's name spoken in a soft, coquettish tone, Leah saw a momentary and unreadable look shadow Rachel's face. Leah felt a queer pang in her heart.

"Jim…" Leah began, not knowing what she would say, and then she gasped, like a character in an old horror movie. Even the gasp was horrifying in the quiet woods as she saw something reach out of the bushes for Rachel.

"What?" Rachel's eyes grew wide and white as she slowly turned, and seeing the grasping hand, screamed… then laughed. She swallowed hard. "It's only a statute," she said, grabbing it at the elbow. Both women laughed loudly with uneasy relief that bordered hysteria.

Rachel turned to head back, and Leah followed, pausing to admire the mushrooms, or were they toadstools? She knelt to pick one. She would ask Rachel, who was nowhere in sight. Upon rising, her right foot tripped over a damp log and she tumbled headfirst through the thicket of rhododendron. She pawed at thin air, surprised and bewildered, for the leaves and branches pulled away from her.

Searing, shocking pain shot through her body as

she tumbled down the rocky cliff. The woods whirled, and she felt a final woofing blow on her head before everything went black, and yet she could see herself running to catch up with Freddie and Norma, like a dream within a dream. They waited by the four stone pillars that rose enchantingly at the end of the meadow. One of the center pillars stood cracked, partly fallen, and the stone lintel above parked precariously askew. Crumbled steps led to a small, much overgrown courtyard.

"Wow! Cool!" Norma said.

"Oh, how pretty," Leah replied.

Freddie had already jumped down into the garden, foregoing the steps.

Leah and Norma made their way down more demurely, exploring the paths and shadowed corners. Here and there were statues, fauns and nymphs emerging from tangled weeds. *It's a fairytale garden,* Leah thought, utterly besotted by it all. At fifteen, few girls her age still loved make-believe, but she preferred the magic and constancy of childhood to make-up, gossip, clothes and boys. Still, watching Freddie, thin and pale, his blond idyllic curls fretted with leaves, swinging a branch and bashing through the weeds like a jungle explorer, she suddenly wished Norma would disappear.

In the middle of the little courtyard was a

fountain, broken, like the steps and tumbled pillars. Atop the fountain, a little cherub held an empty pitcher against his pudgy hip, pouring nothing for eternity. Leah peered up and into the basin which was half full of mossy green water. Two dragonflies, stuck together, fluttered above, the colors of their wings mesmerizing.

Freddie, hear my heart calling. Take my hands before the magical fountain and kiss me.

"Where are those kids?" someone said.

Freddie, bored with the garden, leapt up the steps.

"Come on. Let's get something to eat," Norma said to Leah who stood stock still before the fountain, watching her wishes fly away with the dragonflies.

And then Leah found herself lying beneath a moss-bearded faun that silently piped a voiceless tune from beneath a rhododendron. The puckish face of the faun was worn to softness by time and weather.

Leah tried to move, but every effort was agony.

She lay on her back and her head throbbed like a kettle drum. One arm twisted above her head in an odd position and she couldn't move it. How long had she been there? The blackness called to her again, and when next she looked about, the moon was a perfect pearl beyond the tree tops. It took several minutes to recall what had happened. Panic slowly fought its way to the surface.

Where is Rachel? Did she just leave me here? In an unkind fancy, she imagined Rachel telling Jim some plausible story about losing Leah, leaving Jim and Rachel guileless and free from guilt to begin, *or continue,* their affair. Leah began to cry. Again, she tried to move. Tears of pain overtook those of sorrow.

When the greatest waves of agony subsided, Leah lay still. How long, she couldn't tell. The opalescent moon shifted a little in the small space of sky above. She looked around as best she could. A large stone structure rose above. She reached out with her good arm and felt the cool, pebbled skin of granite. She lay by the base of the pedestal, atop which was a circular basin of sorts. Through the dense underbrush, she spied a pile of five or six lateral stones, crooked and broken. Above them and emerging out of the thickets, she could make out the shadowy form of a Romanesque pillar. Not far from the pillar stood two figures.

"Hello?" Leah cried out.

They paid no heed. More statues? No. They moved closer to one another and clasped hands, intertwining fingers.

Leah could see the face of the boy. He was spectrally white in the moonlight, his face framed by soft blond curls.

Leah blinked, but the figures remained.

The girl's long hair cascaded to the top of the jodhpurs she wore.

Had she unbraided her hair that day? She couldn't remember.

Gently, the boy leaned in and kissed her softly, so softly.

Leah felt tears run down her dirty face.

"Is that what happened? Is this real? Is this real?" she whispered in a damaged mantra. Leah watched the ghosts play, swinging hands, past the steps, past the pillar and into the woods beyond.

Shafts of light swept far above and through the treetops.

"Leah. Leah!" Rachel's voice! Not coy or cool this time, but desperate, cracked and rough. "Leah! Where are you? Answer me."

"Rachel… over here. Watch your step."

* * *

The Path Home
by Jennifer Doss
Previous CWI Contest Winner

"Sissy-boy going home to Mommy?" Jared jumped out from behind a tree and barred Ashley's way.

"Get outta my way," Ashley said.

Bobby rode up on his bicycle. "Or what? Yer gonna cry?" he said, joining in.

Ashley rubbed his bruised ribs from their earlier encounter at school. He wasn't sure he could take another beating. He tucked his head and shoved between the boys.

Jared yanked him back, hard. "We aren't finished with you," he hissed.

Tears flooded Ashley's eyes. He tried to blink them back, but the welling fear forced them over the edge. He shoved, trying to push through.

"We ain't even touched you yet and yer already cryin'," Bobby laughed.

Without looking up, Ashley darted forward and slid around Jared.

Bobby rode full force, slamming into him.

Ashley's ankle twisted unnaturally beneath the bike's tire.

Jared ran up, panting. "Now it's gonna be worse

cuz we had to catch you. Get up!"

"I ca… can't," Ashley whimpered, trying to stand and falling back down.

"Help me, Bobby," Jared said.

Bobby stowed his top of the line bike in an alleyway. If something happened to the bike, his parents wouldn't blink at buying him a newer, fancier one. The rowdies hoisted the smaller boy up and each slung his arm over their shoulder. On a normal day, they towered over Ashley, but his hanging, limp form made him look even smaller and more vulnerable.

Terror gripped Ashley and bile burned the back of his throat. Nothing good could come of this. Ever since his first day at Elmwood Middle School, Jared and Bobby had found him an easy target. Between his name, which they insisted meant he was either transgender or gay, and his scrawny body, he made the perfect victim. Ashley tried to avoid them, but 'accidental' jabs to his ribs and feet came too frequently. As if torturing him at school wasn't enough, they followed him home and shouted obscenities all the way. Ashley changed his route time and again, but somehow Jared and Bobby always found him.

"Where are you taking me?" Ashley said.

"Why, to the hospital, of course. Gotta get that ankle looked at," Jared said, his voice oozing sarcasm.

The situation was worse than Ashley thought. He wrenched his arms away, but collapsed as soon as he tried to stand.

"See? You need our help," Bobby said.

They dragged him toward a densely wooded area. Few people passed, and whenever someone looked concerned, one of the boys would say, "You'll be okay, buddy," or "The doctor will fix you up." Oh yeah? What doctor would be waiting in the woods? Couldn't they tell the kids were insincere? Why didn't someone offer to call a parent or police officer? Most were too wrapped up in their phones to even spare them a glance. If only he had a cell phone of his own. He had begged his parents, but they didn't think he was responsible enough.

The smell of earth and leaves met his nostrils. Civilization had vanished and they were solidly in the woods now.

"Here you go, sissy-boy. You can stay here and cry your little eyes out," Bobby said. "No one will miss you anyway."

"My mom…" Ashley started.

"Mommy might come looking and will probably throw a party when she can't find you. Her life will be easier without having a sissy for a son. Or maybe you're really a girl?" Jared said. "Should we find out?" They dropped him on the ground and reached for his waistband.

"Nah, nobody wants to see that nastiness," Bobby answered, shifting his eyes away.

"How about this instead?" Jared said, as his foot connected with Ashley's groin.

Ashley grunted as the sharp pain made him draw his knees up. He still hadn't caught his breath when more feet flew at him, then came the punches. He rolled into a ball and cried, until mercifully, darkness swallowed him.

When he opened his eyes, fading sunlight streamed through the trees. This wasn't the same place where they had beaten him. Where was he? Gingerly, he poked his body parts. There was pain, but it wasn't excruciating until he tried to stand. His ankle rolled to the side, refusing to hold him up.

"Hello?" he called, hoping Jared and Bobby were long gone. He couldn't imagine what they would do if they heard him. "Hello? I need help!"

No one seemed to be coming. Sunlight streamed through the canopy of trees. Trees he didn't recognize. So majestic. A light, drifting fog reminded him of scenes like this in fantasy movies. Where was he? He had only lived here nine months, so maybe this was some deep part of the woods where they hoped he wouldn't be found. If only he had screamed for help when there were people around. Why hadn't he?

"Help!" he yelled. Minutes ticked by and still he was alone. Ashley dragged himself onto a nearby fallen log. Gingerly, he lifted his damaged ankle and set it on top of the log.

"I am completely and utterly lost. I'm going to die out here," he whispered.

"You are not lost."

Ashley whirled around. A girl emerged, golden hair glowing in the sunlight. She looked to be older than him, though not yet an adult. With her came a sense of calm, covering him like a blanket.

"Well, I don't know where I am or how to get home, so yeah, I'm lost," Ashley explained. The words sounded harsher than his tone. To his surprise, the crippling fear was gone.

"I know the way home," she said.

Her smile disarmed him in every way and though he wanted to distrust her, everything in him was drawn to her.

"What's your name?" he asked.

"Emelia," she said. "What's yours?"

"Ashley."

"Very nice to meet you, Ashley. Come with me. I'll show you the way home." She reached for his hand and without thinking he tried to stand, only to fall back onto the log.

"My ankle. It's hurt. I can't walk. Can you get

help?" he asked.

Without a word, Emelia disappeared from view.

Ashley breathed in the fresh, cool air. The pain grew less intense with each breath, and peace fell over him as the mist settled.

"Let me see your foot," Emelia said.

Ashley nearly toppled off the log in surprise. She had reappeared behind him without a sound. "You didn't get help?" he asked.

"I'll help you," she said, yanking his ankle toward her.

He winced, but only a mild ache throbbed in response.

Emelia took two flat pieces of sturdy bark and framed his ankle, wrapping them with long leaves and using vines to tie it.

"What's all that?" Ashley asked.

"It will make your head feel better."

"My head? What's wrong with my head?" He probed his head, but found no tender spots. He must look disheveled after his altercation. A smile crept up Emelia's face as she watched him comb his hair with his fingers and smooth it down.

"Come," she said, reaching for him.

Tenderly, he placed weight on his ankle and was surprised to find it could bear weight. "Thank you. Where are we going?"

"Home," Emelia said, her golden hair shining like the sun itself. A circle of light ringed her head so brightly, it was difficult to look at.

"Your home?" Ashley said.

Emelia nodded and continued into the forest. The sunlight grew brighter as they walked a narrow, overgrown path. An intricately woven gate rose before them, and the sun seemed to originate from just beyond.

"Here we are," she said.

"Are your parents home?"

"Yes, my Father sent me to get you."

"Your Father sent you? How did he know? Where's your mom?" Ashley asked. Maybe she didn't have a mom, and he inwardly kicked himself for being so insensitive.

She giggled. "My Father knows everything."

"Sure, he does. Then he knows what happened to me?"

"Of course. That's why you're here," she said.

"Did he see them beat me up? Why didn't he stop them? He just left, and then sent you to get me?" There had been a witness, someone who could've stopped Jared and Bobby. But instead of stopping them, he walked away, leaving him bloodied and alone. Tears welled up again. People only cared about themselves.

"Everything will be okay. Father does not intervene, but He knows you. He saved you when you cried for help many years ago. There's a place for you here," Emelia said.

Images flooded Ashley's head.

The narrow, overgrown path. The peacefulness. The halo over Emelia's head. A Father who knew all. A Savior who saved him. A place prepared for him. He really was home.

* * *

Saved by the Belle
by Ronnie Dauber
Previous CWI Contest Winner

When you have a dream that suggests something bad is going to happen, I think it's best to just stay home in bed and let the day pass. But then, when you're the teacher of an eighth-grade class that's expecting you to greet them onboard the school bus, you must ignore your doubts and go anyway.

We'd planned the special trip for months. We would camp overnight at Valens Lake with sixteen students and four adults. We'd fill the days with swimming, canoeing, and hiking and spend the night around a huge campfire roasting weenies and marshmallows and telling ghost stories. No one had any allergies or illnesses, and almost everyone had some kind of camping experience. The plan was flawless.

We were all onboard, chatting and laughing as we waited for Mr. Kerr, our driver, to arrive. Then I spotted our old, burly school principal walking toward the bus, so I stepped outside to greet him.

He sauntered over to me with the usual cynical grin on his face. "Morning, Jake," he said.

I nodded and tried to smile back, but it wasn't

easy as this man had an annoying persona that made me want to tell him to go away and stop trying to ruin my life, but I put on my happy face and greeted him anyway. What he had to say, though, was not what I wanted to hear.

"You'll have to drive this bus, Jake. Bus driver's got the flu, and you're the only one qualified."

I tried to decline, but having an intelligent conversation with this guy was like arguing with the answering machine, so we spent the next twenty minutes going over a hand-drawn map. And before I knew it, I was sitting in the driver's seat, ready to drive a bus I wasn't familiar with, taking a bunch of overzealous teens to a place I'd never been while reading a sketched map that made no sense. There was no time to look for a real map as the ferry sailed at 11 a.m. It was already after 6:30, and it would take at least four hours to get there.

The plan was beginning to show flaws!

The kids cheered and stomped the floor as we pulled onto the main highway. That wasn't a problem as I knew my way around my neck of the woods, but I'd never been to Valens Lake before, and I had no idea what the drive would entail. It would have been so much easier if the bus had been made in this century and equipped with GPS, but our principal was cheap, so I would pretend I knew where I was going.

No one noticed my tremors as flashes of my nightmare flooded my mind and doused my brow with cold beads of sweat. I had to remind myself that I was a competent, middle-aged man who had never been lost in his life. I wasn't about to let a dream that predicted I'd get lost and almost killed change the way people saw me. And by people, I'm really referring to Meagan, the single mother of one of the students who'd come along to help supervise the kids. I wanted to impress her so she'd say yes when I asked her out.

With the help of Mr. Grady, the English teacher, I managed to get to the ferry with ten minutes to spare. It took about an hour to cross, and it was entertaining. On the other side of the river, there were a couple of times when I had no idea where we were, but I got through it without looking lost, and before we knew it, we were at the park.

The attendant came out to greet us. The kids poured out of the bus and watched me park it – an unexpected monumental event that involved backing it between two other buses. After a minute of pleading with God under my breath, I succeeded. I think I impressed Meagan because she gave me a thumbs-up and shouted, "Good job!"

After we'd registered, the camp attendant said they had electrical issues, so we should take a lantern to the washrooms in case the lamplights went out.

Minutes later, we headed to our campsite.

After setting up camp, we brought out the iron pots and warmed up the canned beans and potatoes and enjoyed an old-fashioned campsite meal. Shortly after, we split into teams and went on a hike around the lake, noting the different wildlife and amazing scenery. It was a great adventure, and of course, Meagan's team and mine went together, so that made it even better. We had a chance to get to know each other a bit more, and I did my best to impress her. Everything was going good. If I could keep this up, she'd say yes when I asked her out.

Before we knew it, everyone was sitting around the campfire talking and laughing and snacking and having a great time. I tried to sit where Meagan could join me, but instead, I was blessed with the company of two chatty female students who insisted on teaching me the new chat line on their I-pods.

After drinking a few cans of pop, I needed to go to the little boy's room. In a way, I was glad because I needed an excuse to get away from the annoying girls whose sole purpose was to turn me into a middle-aged cyber pro. I excused myself and took off down the path, not bothering to grab a lantern since I never get lost. Besides that, the lamp posts were lit, and I'd be back before they got to the next verse of "Ninety-nine bottles of pop on the wall."

My walk turned into a run, and I didn't pay attention to anything around me as I was in a bit of a hurry. I made it to the restroom, and life was good again. Seconds later, I was on the path heading back to camp, and that's when the lamps went out! It was then that I wished that I'd not only brought the lantern, but also paid a bit more attention to how I got there.

To say it was dark was an understatement. I pulled out my cell phone and used it as a flashlight, but the shadows it cast made the surroundings look different. Before I knew it, I came to that famous fork in the road that comes with every suspense story, and I hadn't a clue which one led to our camp. I listened for the sounds of voices, but heard none.

I was sure I'd made a slight left turn to get to the bathroom, so I assumed I should turn slightly right to get back. I took the right path, hoping I would get back to camp before I became the full course meal for a nation of mosquitoes. Just when I thought things couldn't get any worse, I heard the distant roll of thunder.

I kept walking slowly and, of course, could not see the tree root that spread across the path. I tripped, and the phone flew out of my hands as a crack of lightning lit the sky. The eerie shadows fed my wild imagination as heavy thunder shook the ground.

Luckily, I could see the phone because of its

light, so I crawled to get it and then stood up, totally lost. I didn't want to get caught in the oncoming storm. I walked a bit further, and could *not* believe my eyes. There were paths going in every direction, and any minute, I would be fried by lightning or drowned by a torrential rain.

In my frustration, I began to shout. "I don't believe this. I am completely and utterly lost! I'm going to die out here if you don't help me!" I was hoping God would feel sorry for me and flip the lights back on or at least show me the way back to camp. Instead, I heard a crackling sound on the path behind me that sent shivers up my spine. I'm a guy, and I don't scare easily, but this was one of those rare occasions when my knees grew weak. I took a deep breath and yelled in what turned out to be a wimpy voice, "Who's there?"

Suddenly, the sky lit up again, and I saw the silhouette of someone walking toward me. Oh, how I wish we hadn't just told a bunch of creepy ghost stories! I tried to call for help, but the only thing that came out of my mouth was a pathetic squeak. The figure drew closer. My heart pounded in my ears. I held my breath and waited.

Then I heard, "Jake, is that you?"

I tried to be brave, so I opened one eye. "Meagan Jones?"

"Um, I guess that's me. I'm on my way back from the girl's room, and the power just went out."

I knew it would be stretching my hopes a bit to think that she hadn't just heard my childish scream for help, so I cleared my throat and tried to sound confident. "I was just fooling around and yelled that out. I'm okay, really. But you look lost."

She giggled and said she wasn't lost because she'd been here before and she knew the way back. Then she added that the storm looked like it would bypass us.

Through the soft glow of the lantern I saw her sweet smile. I knew we had connected.

"By the way," she said, "my name is Isabelle Meagan-Jones, but you can call me Belle."

I don't know if God has a sense of humor or if He was just teaching me something, but my ego took a sudden plunge.

She leaned in close and whispered, "This will be our little secret. If you won't tell anyone that you got lost, I won't tell them you got saved by the Belle."

When she slipped her small, delicate hand in mine, I wanted to dance all the way back to camp.

* * *

Plain Old Regular
by Karen Rush
Previous CWI Contest Winner

"You know what, Pop? I'm getting tired of your saying you're lonely. You don't want to be by yourself? Then get out there. You've got what, three women after you?"

Dominic shrugged, regretting he had said anything.

"I can name at least three," Joan said, counting on her fingers. "Betty, Iris, and oh, what's her name...?" She glanced around her kitchen as if the refrigerator or dishwasher would spark her memory. "Ah, Dora. That's it. Dora. Humph. Any one of them would be thrilled, *thrilled*, if you paid the slightest bit of attention to them."

"Eh."

"Don't you 'eh' me," she said, as she tapped his shoulder. "Come on. What's wrong with Betty?"

"Bingo Betty?" Dominic wrinkled his nose. "Smoke and nachos."

"What?"

"She smells like a bingo hall, all smoke and nachos." He ran his hand through the few grey strands of remaining hair. "Then the other day? I asked if I could borrow a pen, so I could write a check at Wal-Mart, and you know what she does? She reaches into her purse and pulls out one of those inky, binky, bingo dauber things. What was I supposed to do with that?"

"Wait. You took her to Walmart?"

"Yeah, Sunday morning. It's not crowded then."

"Okay," Joan said, shaking her head. "There are a lot of reasons that's wrong, but we won't go into that now. What about Iris?"

"Church lady? Flowers. She smells too much like flowers. She plants flowers at church, sets flowers on the altar, delivers flowers to the sick and sad. Flowers, flowers, flowers."

"But that's all good, right?"

"Are you kidding me? Flowers smell too much like funerals. Your mother's."

"Oh gosh, I guess that's understandable." Joan began to clear dishes from the table. "So, what about Dora? What does she smell like?"

"Desperation. Like I'm her last hope."

"You're unbelievable."

"Can I help it if your mother's a hard act to follow? No malarkey with her. She was real. Said what she thought and kept me in line, too. Sometimes a man needs that. Not like all these old clingy biddies that *yes* me to death. I'm tired of it." He sat quietly for a moment, and then pulled a wrinkled handkerchief from his back pocket and dabbed his eyes and nose. He cleared his throat. "Okay. Enough yammering already. How about you offer your old man some coffee before he heads home?"

Joan glanced at the clock. "It's kind of late."

"Not for me. I can always drink coffee."

"Okay, I'll make it while you wipe off the table, deal?" She handed him a dish cloth.

"Deal. It's the least I can do since you fed me." He wiped the table, brushed the crumbs and little pieces of lettuce onto the floor.

"Oh, Pop, don't…"

"Aw, keep your shirt on, I'm gonna sweep."

"Really? You know how to sweep?"

"Of course. I learned how to do a lot of things since your mother died. It's not like she left me with a lifetime supply of clean underwear, ya know. I can take care of myself."

"Well, it's been three years now." Joan leaned against the counter and crossed her arms as she watched. "I have to admit, I'm impressed with how well you're doing, considering how perpetually grouchy you are."

"I'm not grouchy. Quit saying I'm grouchy all the time. I can be fun, when the mood strikes me."

"Oh? Okay." Joan bit the insides of her cheeks to hide the grin tickling the corners of her mouth.

"And you forgot one," he said.

"One what?"

"Stalker. There are four. Not three."

"Oh, Pop, I wouldn't exactly call those old ladies *stalkers*."

"Well, I would. And Casserole Carol is the worst."

At that very moment, *Casserole Carol* sat on the edge of her bed in the spare room of her sister's house. Carol wore a new shade of pink lipstick and her best blouse from Sears.

This is the last time I'm taking Dominic food, she thought. She was beginning to feel ridiculous and doubted he was a good catch anyway. She took one last glance in the mirror. Her reflection surprised her. Who was that old woman? "I guess it's time to go see the old grump," she said to her sister, as she walked into the kitchen.

"Who?" Margaret stood holding the casserole she had just taken out of the oven.

"*Who?* Dominic, as if you didn't know, the neighborhood grouch that lives across the street." Carol plopped down on a kitchen chair. "I don't know if I'm up to this anymore. I don't think he likes me."

"What's not to like? Just keep smiling and complimenting him. He'll come around."

"Around for what?"

"Around to move you out of my spare room. I want to put my crafts back in there," Margaret said, smiling, and then hummed the wedding march as she pressed foil over the top of the casserole.

Carol stared at her back. She could hardly breathe, and it was moments before she could even speak. "You're kicking me out? I'm seventy-three years old and you're trading me for crafts? With casseroles? To a curmudgeon?" Carol laid her head on the kitchen table and hid her face in her arms, then lifted her head to glare at Margaret. "For cryin' out loud, stop being so perky. And you know what? I hate your apron, especially the stupid gingham ruffled one. No one wears aprons anymore. They died with June Cleaver."

"Well, well, aren't you the testy one today? Never mind, stand up and let me look at you." Margaret pulled Carol to her feet. "Go on. Twirl around. Hmm. Not bad, but you should cover up some of that grey. She tried to fluff Carol's hair as the latter squirmed away. "Some perfume, maybe?"

"No."

"Air freshener?"

"Not funny."

"Oh, alright then," Margaret said, as she scooped up a small bottle from the kitchen counter. "I'll just dab a little vanilla behind your ears, just to sweeten the pot."

Ten minutes later, Carol knocked on Dominic's front door until her hand hurt. Each knuckle-bruising rap made her more irritable. She'd stood there enough times to know he had disconnected his doorbell and would not answer unless she was persistent. She glanced across the street and caught a glimpse of her sister peering through the living room window.

Margaret grinned and gave a thumb's up.

Carol muttered profanities and put her hand up to rap again… just as Dominic's door opened.

"Oh, you again." He scratched his belly.

It took all of her energy just to look at him. She knew she should smile and say something cute, but it wasn't coming.

He stared back. His shirt was buttoned cockeyed, his hair stood on end as if he'd been napping, and he wore dirty, corduroy house slippers with black socks. "So, what ya got this time?" He stifled a yawn, and then leaned toward her and sniffed.

"Ugh, stop," she said, pulling away abruptly, jerking the casserole to her chest. Its sudden heat startled her, and she gasped as it fell to the pavement and shattered.

"Well, that was clever," Dominic said as he put his hands in his pockets and snickered.

Carol surveyed the sloppy, steaming mess. Her

legs stung where the sauce had splattered, but seeing the gravy soaked noodles stuck to Dominic's pants and slippers made up for it. She picked a slick brown mushroom off her skirt and flicked it at him. "Well, Dominic, I hope this casserole wasn't one of your favorites."

"I don't know, smells okay. What was it?"

"I have absolutely no idea and I really, really don't care. Ask my sister. I'll bet she's watching right now." Without turning, Carol pointed over her shoulder with her thumb. "If the curtains move, that's her. She makes all these stupid casseroles and sends me over here to flirt with you."

"Yeah?"

"Yeah, and either I don't know how to flirt anymore, or you're an idiot. Maybe both, because I'm pretty sure you're an idiot either way." She shrugged. "It doesn't matter. So long Dominic. I'm not doing this anymore." She kicked a large chunk of broken glass aside. "Don't bother returning the dish."

Dominic leaned on the doorframe as he watched her walk away. Suddenly, he straightened up and tried to pat down his unruly hair. When she reached the curb, he called to her. "Hey, Carol, wanna go out for coffee?"

She turned, amazed. "What?"

"My daughter says that's what people do

nowadays. They go to fancy coffee places. Personally, I like getting' the senior discount at McDonald's, but she says that's not good enough. And I hope you don't need anything from Walmart because that's off limits, too."

"No."

"No? You don't wanna go?" He threw his hands in the air. "Gosh, with all those casseroles and the flirting, I thought…"

"No. I meant going for coffee is good, and no, I don't need anything from Walmart."

Dominic nodded. "Okay, so let's go. You drive."

The coffee shop buzzed around them as Dominic led the way to the counter.

Couples huddled around small tables in scattered conversations while jazzy music played in the background. Laptops were open and cell phones were glowing as a camaraderie of youthful vigor permeated.

Carol wished she had wiped some of the gravy off her legs.

"Boy, this place is busy, but at least it smells good, huh?" Dominic said. They stood side by side staring at the menu bolted to the wall.

"Yes, it smells heavenly, but holy cow, have you ever seen such a big chalkboard in all your life?"

"That's pretty darn big and they sure got a lotta

stuff written on it." Dominic felt his back pocket, reassuring himself that he had his wallet.

A slender man with a loose bun on the top of his head waited behind the shiny granite counter. He wore skinny black jeans and held a marker in one hand and an oversized paper cup in the other. He squelched a sigh as he watched Carol and Dominic. "You two ready to order?"

"Oh, just a moment, please," Carol said, not taking her eyes off the board. Colorfully chalked capital and lower-case letters interspersed with an artistic flair that made the menu seem pert and happy. Some items had broad squiggly boxes drawn around them. Others were underlined a few times, as if though they were a bit more important. The dollar signs were uniform and tiny, the prices large.

"Ma'am? Uh, we're kinda busy," Man Bun said, tapping one foot.

Carol gave him a grim smile as she clutched her purse under her arm. People crowded in close, and she felt the uncomfortable heat of their eagerness. Her neck stiffened, and she wondered if her brain was experiencing some sort of glitch. She turned to Dominic in frustration.

"I am completely and utterly lost."

"What?"

"I don't see coffee up there. Do you see coffee

up there?"

Dominic glanced back at the board. "Frappucino, Cappucino, Latte, Espresso... that's not even English, is it?"

"Honestly? I don't know."

"Say, buddy," Dominic said, as he pointed to the board. "Which one of those is coffee?"

Man Bun smiled. "All of it is coffee. Gourmet."

"Gourmet, huh? That's what all those fancy words are? Gourmet? We don't want that. We want…"

"Look, if this is new to you, let me suggest a grande blonde roast."

"Huh? No, no blondes," Dominic said, as he nodded his head toward Carol.

"A shot of espresso, then? Or I could make that a latte, even a skinny latte… for the lady?"

Dominic looked at Carol. "You want that?"

"I don't know. This is all new to me. Young man, what else do you suggest?"

"If you like a sweet drink, we could go with a caramel cappuccino." He began to hit the marker against the cup with short, sharp, rhythmic taps.

Carol nodded. "Okay, yes, I guess that will do."

"Tall, grande, or venti?"

She shrugged.

"We'll make it grande. Wet or dry?"

Carol leaned into Dominic. "What in the world is he talking about?"

"Darned if I know. I just want a cup of coffee and coffee's wet. Let me take care of this." He held Carol's elbow, nudging her out of the way, and then slapped his hand on the counter. "Buddy, we've decided. We want two wet." He turned back to Carol and grinned.

"Two wet... *what*?" Man Bun asked, smiling at the server beside him who laughed softly and rolled his eyes.

"Hey, I saw that," Dominic said. "Look, all's I want is two coffees. Two plain old regular coffees, and you can make them as wet as you want."

"Drip medium or dark roast?"

Dominic leaned into the counter. "Two *regular* coffees," he said, as he thumbed through his wallet. He pulled out his driver's license and laid it on the counter. "*And* a senior discount."

"Okay, I give up," Man Bun said. "I'll make that special for you, but no discount. Alright?"

"Yeah, okay."

"And don't go telling all your friends either. I don't need a geriatric stampede in here."

Before Dominic could reply, a young man in a plaid shirt inched his way forward. "Excuse me, sir. Do you mind if I go ahead and order? I've got to get back to work."

"Naw, go ahead." Dominic stepped aside.

"Thanks." He shook Dominic's hand, as he called to the server. "Espresso macchiato."

Two giggly girls in school uniforms followed him. "Okay if we order, too?"

Dominic nodded and motioned them ahead.

"I'll have a salted caramel mocha, please."

"And a grande iced coffee with extra whipped cream," the other said.

"Say, are you girls old enough to drink coffee?" Dominic said.

The first girl held up a ring of keys and shook them. "Well, I'm old enough to drive so I guess so, but Grandpa says this isn't really coffee anyway. At least not for *real* coffee drinkers."

"Yeah? Your grandpa sounds like a smart man."

"He is," she said. "You kind of remind me of him." She looked at Dominic's disheveled hair, and then not knowing where else to look, her eyes fell on his slippers. She glanced away and giggled.

"Order up. Plain old regular," Man Bun said.

Dominic raised his hand and then turned to Carol. "Come on, that's us."

"No." She took his arm. "Let's leave."

"But, that's us."

"No, it's not. Look. " She held out her gravy

stained skirt and then pointed to her splattered legs. "And you… look how your shirt is buttoned. And your socks are saggy. And you didn't even wear shoes. Honestly."

Dominic stared at his slippers.

"And then a man calls out, 'Plain old regular,' and you answer that it's us? Look at us, Dominic. We are anything but plain, old *or* regular and we are *not* marching up to the counter and taking two cups of it." Her breath caught, and she looked away. Her shoulders began to shake.

Dominic hesitated. "Aw, Carol," he said, as he touched her arm. She turned to him and his heart lurched when he saw her tears. It was a moment before he realized she couldn't stop… giggling? "Carol?"

She took a deep breath to steady herself just when the barista called out again, "Plain, old and regular."

"Huh," Dominic said, glancing around. "Wonder who that poor sap is?"

He grinned when Carol snorted. "Hey, girl, can you pull yourself together to drive?" he asked, steering her toward the exit.

"Sure," she said, "and I'm going to McDonalds for coffee. Want to come?"

A young couple hurried past them and thanked

Dominic for holding the door. He smiled and nodded, but his eyes were on Carol. She smelled like fresh-baked cookies.

* * *

Sea Princess
by Autumn Fenton
Previous CWI Contest Winner

"Cyrus Stone was reading a western when the yelling started outside. He tented the book face-down on the coffee table, hobbled over to the window and separated the dusty plastic blind with two fingers. Just as he had feared, the worst had finally happened. Now everyone knew. He squeezed his eyes shut and stood there swaying. He had to go out there.

Cyrus opened the metal door of the mobile home and stepped onto his deck. He blinked against the lemony summer sun. The briny air caught in his throat, so he swallowed twice, and then moistened his lips.

Maggie Caldwell shook her fist. "We'll slap him with a lawsuit," she shouted. "We're not gonna take this."

The other residents surged around her, nodding approval. Several cursed. The young mother who worked at Walmart shredded the letter. "You got that right!" she said, casting the paper fragments with both hands.

Cyrus watched one jagged piece of paper sail into the patch of red geraniums. He stepped off the deck and stooped down to pluck it from the flower bed. Rolling it into a tight ball, he edged closer to the group and cleared his throat.

The commercial crabber, the one with the loud motorcycle, glared at Cyrus. "You must know something." He planted himself directly in front of Cyrus. "You've been the maintenance man here for something like a hundred years."

"All I know is, Joe said the new owner promised to keep the Sea Princess a mobile home park," Cyrus said. "Apparently, Mr. Rutledge went back on his word."

The crabber shoved his nose into Cyrus' face. "And did you know we only have 90 days to get out?"

"Of course not. I didn't even think we'd have to leave."

Maggie stepped between the two men. "Aw, come on now. That's not very nice. Don't take it out on Mr. Stone."

"But that old dude never talks to any of us."

"What's that have to do with anything? Maybe he just doesn't have much to say. Maybe he…"

Cyrus turned away and walked back into his mobile home. *I have more to lose than any of you,* he thought, *and so does Emily.* He grabbed his book, but couldn't focus, so he slammed it shut. Pacing back and forth, he peered outside every few minutes, waiting for them to leave, and they disappeared as suddenly as they had gathered. Cyrus ventured back outside to water the geraniums.

Maggie must have been watching because she approached before he even unrolled the hose. "I got elected as the Main Cheese in fighting this thing." She fluffed her hair in a pretend preen, then grinned. "Everyone claims it's because I'm so organized, but I think it's really because I have a big mouth."

"What's your plan, Maggie?"

"I just called Rutledge's office, but the snooty secretary said he isn't taking calls from the Sea Princess, so a bunch of us are gonna storm The Rut's office. Isn't that a good name for him? I just made that up."

"I don't know if that's such a good idea," Cyrus said.

Maggie pulled the hose from his hand and tossed it in the grass. "Come on. Everyone is getting ready. We're leaving in five minutes."

"I'm staying here. I have work to do. Plus, I don't think it'll help."

"But you *must* go," Maggie said. "You've lived here forever. In fact, I heard you used to own this place."

Cyrus frowned. "It was only a farm back then," he said slowly. Picking up the hose again, he edged away from Maggie, aimed the nozzle at the flowers, then dropped it by his side.

"Well, I believe we can save this place," Maggie said, "but we won't know until we try. Let's go, my friend."

Most of the residents abandoned the plan after being turned away at the lobby, but the crabber stayed until the security guard escorted them outside. He pumped Maggie's hand. "I got the biggest kick out of you badgering that receptionist," he said. He winked at Cyrus. "Maggie had that poor girl sweatin' putty balls."

"They only think they got rid of us," Maggie said. "Me and Cyrus will wait for him in the parking lot. It's almost lunchtime. He'll leave to go somewhere fancy. No bag lunch for The Rut."

Cyrus exhaled a long breath and followed Maggie to a wrought iron bench stationed near the main door.

"I Googled him," she said. "He builds condos up and down the east coast. He probably figures on building a super fancy and expensive one here because it's so close to the ocean."

"Yes, it's a beautiful location," Cyrus said.

"Yeah. And apparently, he's estranged from his own kids. Do you have family? I never see anyone visiting you."

"No, I'm alone."

"I have three kids and five grandkids. But they never call or visit." Maggie twirled one finger in an ornate loop of the bench. "I'm starved. I would've brought snacks if I'd known we would be on a stakeout."

Cyrus shifted on the bench. "Maybe it isn't such a great idea to approach him out here."

"The jerk better not make me miss my soaps. Do you watch any... there he is! I'll run over there and stand in front of his vehicle so he can't drive off. You nab him."

"What? No." Cyrus gaped as Maggie ran toward the BMW. "Wait... well, okay."

Cyrus walked over to the car, glanced at Maggie, then rested his palm on the hood. "Excuse me, Mr. Rutledge. My name is Cy..."

Rutledge sliced the air with his hand. "I know exactly who you are. You Sea Princess people better stop pestering me." He yanked the door open. "It's a done deal. And you, Mr. Stone, of all people, need to get your stuff out of there. You know what I mean."

"My stuff?" Cyrus grabbed the side of the door. "My *stuff!* How dare you."

Rutledge started the car, threw it into reverse and stepped on the gas. The door flapped wide for a moment, then slammed shut on its own.

Cyrus stood in place. He didn't notice Maggie standing next to him until she touched his hand.

"Geez, I thought The Rut was gonna run over your foot."

Cyrus twisted his mouth to one side. "Stuff. My stuff."

"Are you okay, Cyrus?"

"My Emily."

"What are you talking about? Who is Emily?" She cocked her head to look at his face, noticing new bumps. "Are those hives?"

Cyrus fingered one of the welts on his cheek. It was time to tell her, but not here and not now. He dropped his hand. "He isn't going to win."

"We'll get him at the city council meeting tomorrow. Let's go back to my place, Cyrus. I'll fry up some crab cakes and we'll figure out what to say."

After dinner, they jotted down a number of points to address. When discussing the environmental issues, Cyrus told Maggie how peaceful the area had been before development started.

"Our city was a small town back then," he said. "And our farm was so quiet you could almost hear the buzz of dragonfly wings." He followed Maggie to the sink, and picked up a towel to dry the dishes. As he rubbed the towel over and over on the same spot, he decided to tell her more.

"Emily was my wife. My princess." Cyrus tossed the towel on the kitchen counter. He turned to face Maggie. "Back then, it was fairly common to bury loved ones on your farmland. I wanted her to remain close to me forever."

"The geraniums. She's there, isn't she?"

"Yes. Rutledge wants me to exhume and relocate her body. Or as he put it, get my 'stuff' out of here."

They stared at each other for a moment.

Maggie shook her head. "He can't do that. We won't let him."

Cyrus nodded.

The next afternoon, Maggie led the others into town hall.

Cyrus attempted to open the door for her, but it slipped and smacked his shoulder with a loud thud.

"Whoa," Maggie said. "Are you okay?"

Cyrus wiped his wet palms against his trousers. "I think so."

The residents of the Sea Princess filed into the room, packing two whole rows. Maggie signed in as their designated speaker. Tucking one arm behind her back, she bowed to the group. "Maggie the Mouth at your service," she said. She giggled at their laughter, curtsied in various directions, then plopped down next to Cyrus in the front row.

Cyrus studied Rutledge and his attorney and then each of the council members. Leaning toward Maggie, he cupped his hand over his mouth. "It might be a good idea to address most of your remarks to Sutton. From what I've read about him, he's most sympathetic to the little guy."

"Okay." Maggie fingered her index cards. One pinged out of her hand, but she didn't notice. "It sure is a big turn-out."

"Yes, isn't it great?" Cyrus retrieved the card and handed it to her.

"It's hot in here. Is the AC not working?" Maggie fanned herself with the index cards. "Do you think this is going to be on that public cable station or the news?"

Cyrus twisted toward the camera to check out the call letters. "It's the media."

The cards popped out of Maggie's hand and skidded across the floor. They both glanced down, then back at the conference table as the chairman opened the meeting.

Cyrus scooped up the cards and handed them to Maggie, just as the chairman called her name.

Maggie shuffled the cards. Some were upside down. Some were backwards. All were out of sequence. Her eyes bulged. "I am completely and utterly lost." She shoved the cards toward him. "I can't do this."

The chairman tapped the microphone. "Margaret Caldwell," he said again.

"You don't need your notes. You got this nailed."

"No. I can't do this. I don't know what to say." Maggie hunched down in her chair. "You have to do it."

Cyrus swiveled his body toward her, his mouth forming a capital O.

"Last call. Margaret Caldwell. Sea Princess."

Maggie's eyes darted in panic. "Please," she said in a whisper.

Cyrus snapped his mouth shut. Standing on wobbly legs, he walked toward the front.

The chairman boomed. "Well, hello there, Miss Caldwell. Or should I say Mrs.?" The audience tittered.

Cyrus clutched the sides of the podium to maintain balance. His fingers fused to something sticky. *Too many sweaty palms,* he thought. The smell of moth balls from his suit wafted into his face, making him sneeze. The faces of the panel seemed to glob together like masks in a horror film. He blinked twice and planted his feet, and then forced himself to look at each member separately. It worked.

They looked like actual people now. Most wore

a neutral expression, but some still grinned. Rutledge smirked.

"My name is Cyrus Stone." He glanced at the panel.

Rutledge leaned back in his chair.

Cyrus looked away from him. "I've done my research. This property has *not* been rezoned. You are evicting us without a guarantee that it can be developed."

The audience clapped. Cyrus's mouth tasted like a lizard wiggling in desert sand. None of the panel smiled now.

"Our mobile homes were grandfathered in before the current Federal regulations." He stared at the panel again. "In addition, there is very little low-income housing in this area, so you are forcing us out and we have no place to go."

Rutledge pressed his elbows down against the arms of the chair and whispered something to his attorney.

"The Sea Princess is home to rabbits, ducks and geese. Sometimes you see an occasional deer, or even a fox. I discovered a nest of Piping Plovers there last week. We all know these feisty little shorebirds were on the threatened list for a decade or so. You can't destroy endangered species without upsetting nature!"

Rutledge's attorney leaned forward to speak.

"My client is willing to offer each tenant the equivalent of six month's rent if they agree to vacate within the original time frame. This is a generous offer. State law does not require relocation compensation."

The audience was instantly silenced, but then just as quickly started murmuring.

Cyrus felt like a gunslinger in the Old West. Narrowing his eyes, he took aim. "We don't want your money. We want our homes. We want our community."

The audience erupted in cheers and applause, stomping feet and whooping.

Cyrus' face flamed with empowerment. He pounded the podium. "Keep your stinkin' money! We will never leave our homes," he yelled, and the crowd went crazy.

The chairman tapped his microphone several times. "Everyone settle down. We will not tolerate these disruptions." He covered the microphone with one hand and huddled with several of the panel members, then angled his body toward the audience. "This issue is complex. We will notify you of any more schedule meetings. Meeting adjourned."

The other residents rushed over to congratulate Cyrus. He fist-bumped the crabber and high-fived the Walmart mom. A young couple he didn't recognize offered a thumbs-up, and he returned it. Then Maggie was standing next to him.

"Sorry I flaked out on you," she said, "but you did a fabulous job!"

"It's going to be a fight to the bitter end," he said.

"Some of them are going to take the money and run," Maggie said. "Maybe most of them."

"I know."

"Then everyone will go their separate ways."

"That's probably true," Cyrus said, "but for now, it's one day at a time. I've got to get back there to fix those loose boards on the pier. There's lots of summer still left."

Four months passed, and scarlet leaves skidded across freshly-mounded brown earth. Zipping his jacket, Cyrus tilted his head toward the yolk-yellow sun. He nodded at Father O'Malley and bowed his head, but Father O'Malley closed his prayer book. Cyrus turned to see what had caught the priest's attention.

Both watched the procession of cars round the bend and climb the hill. One by one, the vehicles parked in a single row.

Maggie stepped out of hers first. She lifted a pot of red geraniums from the back seat, held them up for Cyrus to see and then clutched them tight against her chest. She waved the other arm in a wide arc.

Cyrus' face broke into a broad smile as he waved back. "My friends are here," he said. "Now Emily will rest in peace. Let me say hi to them and we can begin."

* * *

It's in the Bag
by Constance Lindgreen
CWI Contest Finalist 2017 & Judge's Pick

Half the money's in the bag. That's what it said in Uncle Paul's note, according to the lawyer. So... where's the other half?

It was actually a pretty clever way to get me to come to the funeral. When the lawyer called, I thought it might be about the alimony payments. I was about to claim I was just the plumber and hang up, but then I remembered I'd already put the money into Susan's account. Between the payments to her and the bill from my mother's nursing home, my salary doesn't go very far. Pizza, Chinese food, sometimes a Starbucks.

Uncle Paul had lots, from when he owned the cement business. The schmo with the dough, Dad called him. No millionaire, but still... He and Aunt Alice used to take nice holidays--even went to Europe once. Uncle Paul gave a bundle to cancer research people after she died.

That's gotta be the funeral home right there. Yup. Some parking lot! But I guess they've got a captive clientele. We've all gotta go sometime. Seems like a weird place to hand out the goodies. Don't they usually do that at the lawyer's office? Probably one of

Uncle Paul's "things." Crazy guy, but I really liked him.

"Welcome to Tucker's, sir. Please (ahem) accept our condolences on your loss." That was a discreet cough if I ever heard one. Black suit, black tie, shiny black shoes. Spooky! But at least it means I'm in the right place on the right day. The place is creepy. You'd think that green paint would be enough to turn a live-wire moldy. What'd he say? Across the hallway into the Morning Room? Pretty good: morning, mourning... ha ha.

"Benedict? I'm Lesley White, your late uncle's attorney."

Lesley's natty. I'm not. Serious handshake, too. Ouch!

"Do you prefer to be called Ben?"

Um, yeah - actually, I do. Good guess, Les.
"Yeah."

"Ben, it's a little unusual, but we're going to do the reading and distribution right before the funeral itself. I hope you won't mind. Just take a seat."

The sofa's already occupied by my cousins. We aren't big on hugging in my family so I just say 'hi' and wave. Marilyn looks as if she might cry. Paul Junior's inspecting his shoes, and Dotty--well, she lives up to her name, in my humble opinion. All three look bored.

The chairs are surprisingly comfortable for being fake leather. Must've taken a lot of Naugas to make all that hide, huh? There's a ladies' handbag on one of the seats – pink crocodile, if you can believe it! I guess the owner has gone to the ladies room.

Lesley the Lawyer jumps right in. Blah, blah, blah, about my cousins. Lots of dough. A bequest to the Cancer Society. I expected that. And now, hey, he's talking to me.

"Ben, your uncle has left you a small bequest, too. Some of it is in cash. He also left a note which he wanted read to you: "Ben, you're the only one in the family who shares my love of puns and riddles."

He was right about that. The others have zero sense of humor. Paul Jr. and Marilyn are rolling their eyes. Discreetly, of course, out of respect for their dear departed daddy. Okay, I'm waiting.

"So, here's one last riddle: Half the money is in the bag."

Huh? I am completely and utterly lost.

Lesley White, Esquire, presents me with the purse. "Your uncle's bequest, Ben."

My cousins are having a good laugh over Uncle Paul's legacy to me. Ha ha. Very funny. Didn't know pink was my color, et cetera, et cetera. I put it on my lap and fiddle with the flaps and the lock. Sure enough, there's money inside. Lots! Whoa! A note on the lawyer's stationery says it contains $75,000. I'm probably grinning more than I should, but I can't help it. Well, that's a surprise. No other clues, though.

My cousins are being herded into the funeral parlor's Ministry Room to be administered to, I bet. Lesley-the-Lawyer notices me sneaking out. He waylays me. "Your uncle's note was oddly punctuated."

Sure enough. It says, 'Half the money is - in - the bag.' He smirks. Like he just made some kind of joke. Well, okay, Lesley. Thanks, I guess... I'm outta here. Got to get to the bank before it closes.

This is gonna take some explaining, even though Lesley gave me a bunch of papers to show everything's legit. I ask to see the bank manager. Hey, my lucky day. Good-looking lady banker! She's all business, but she warms up when I show her the cash.

"What do I do with the dough?"

"It's up to you, Mister Nesbit, but as your, ah, financial advisor, I'd recommend you invest in a Certificate of Deposit." She looks longingly at my handbag. "And a safe-deposit box."

For what? She stares at the bag, leans forward like she'd like to touch it. Likes pink, I guess. Maybe I should give it to her. I give it a shove in her direction. "Whaddaya think? Would you like to have it?"

"Would I? A Hermes Birkin bag like that..."

She sighs. "At least $110,000."

What a hoot! The bag's the loot. Clever, Uncle Paul. Thanks for giving me the last laugh!

* * *

Silence
by Kim Kluxen Meredith
CWI Contest Finalist 2017

"Help me die." But the words did not register a sound. His parched lips struggled to repeat the urgent plea.

My heart accepted the message. My head did not. *I am completely and utterly lost.*

This is not my world. My world moves. My world is noisy. The people in my world live in a two-story house with a swing set in the backyard and harbors a Cairn terrier named Harry who rings a bell to be walked.

My forty-four-year-old husband rotated from side to side on the white creased sheets of his mechanical hospital bed in the neuro-intensive care unit. Tangled tubes transported liquid nourishment. Another set deposited his waste in clear plastic bags. A motor pumped oxygen into his collapsed lungs through a port in his neck. The machines competed for space in the cramped room. Their monitors blinked and buzzed. I didn't understand their language. My nose filled with unfamiliar hospital odors. My eyes fixated on my husband's scrubbed face.

I am completely and utterly lost.

The layout of the urban hospital annoyed me.

The maze of hallways confused me. I wanted to run away, but the exits were hiding. The elevator rarely appeared, lingering on lower floors for strangers. All the rooms looked the same.

When David asked me to be his voice, I briefly looked away. I did not want to let my face show my fear. In a moment, I turned back and smiled and stroked his cheek. The muscles of his face were his only outlet for movement. He opened his mouth and wrapped his tongue around my index finger and the warmth of his saliva comforted me.

Two weeks prior to that request, a single-car accident severed his spinal cord and left my dear husband a quadriplegic. His limbs were lifeless. My children's father could not speak. But his mind was as sharp as the broken fragments of his cervical vertebrae.

Four hours passed and I came back with a response.

"Don't worry dear. Joe and I arranged a meeting with the Hospital Ethics Committee. I will be your voice, and I'll carry your message." I tried to sound confident, but I wasn't. It was fortunate that David's former legal mentor, Joe, still practiced in the city and came to my aid after my frantic phone call that day. The well-connected attorney provided the runway, but I was still the driver.

David and I knew our time together on earth was over. We had been preparing ourselves to say goodbye since he was transferred a week ago to the East Coast Regional Spinal Center in Philadelphia. Now our fate was coming into view. We accepted it. It was as though we were having a casual conversation in our family room as we made his final arrangements. We selected the hymns for his funeral. The service would be at our Lutheran Church. He knew the pastor would comfort me. He even suggested I have a luncheon afterwards in the Parish House. It all seemed so perfect on the outside, but inside my head, thoughts battled and bounced around like steel orbs in a pin ball machine.

I am completely and utterly lost.

Cables ushered the cube upwards. I exited on the twelfth floor when the metal doors parted. In front of me, the winter's afternoon sunshine blasted out of the wide entrance of the double oak doors. The amber glare projected through the wall of windows in the room and bounced off the massive oak conference table in the center. The intense sunlight blinded me for a moment. When my vision cleared, a backdrop of 14 men seated in high back leather chairs appeared. Like real-life chess pieces poised next to a wooden board, the figures stood in unison when I entered.

This was not a game. This was a matter of life

and death. My husband's.

I reached in my purse for the 3x5 copy of a recent family photo and took a deep breath. Once I was seated, I lay the creased family photo on the table in front of me and folded my hands. My damp palm stuck to the picture.

"I am here today to ask you to let my husband die with dignity," I said.

My audience's expressions did not change. Immediately I felt an air of skepticism fill the space like a rising flood, and I was sinking.

"David made sure his clients had advanced directives, but he never managed to write his own. We were too busy raising a ten and twelve-year old, but now we both know our time together has run out. I appreciate all that you have done to keep him alive, but it's time to let him go. He has made this request. Please."

The chiseled faces didn't react. My voice echoed in the cavernous room. They were listening, but did they hear me?

Compelled to humanize my husband, I tried to describe our wonderful life together. "My husband once came home with six crystal goblets as payment for a will. His client could not pay the fee. We taught Sunday School together for six years."

They just stared.

"David once made an ark out of pipe cleaners and a paper plate. The kids loved it."

No one spoke.

"This is the first time we have been away from each other. I don't like sleeping alone."

No impression. Their stares bore holes in my face like lasers on target.

I talked for two hours

The Chairmen finally spoke. In a deep, authoritative voice, he dismissed me, saying the Hospital Ethics Committee would inform me of their decision. No one else said a word.

I put my picture back in my purse and stood up. "Thank you," I said meekly. That was all I had left.

I am completely and utterly lost.

The elevator glided down seven stories. When the door opened, the on-duty ICU nurse rushed towards me.

"David's heart stopped beating about ten minutes ago, but it restarted on its own."

He was waiting for me.

I bent over his bed. "I did the best I could. I asked them to please let you die with the dignity you deserve. I think they listened. They will make a decision soon."

David's eyes didn't blink. His gaze fixated on the ceiling.

The nurse explained that he was in a semi-comatose state but that he could still hear me. Five minutes later, the once jagged blue line on the largest monitor near his head flattened out, and a low hum vibrated the cart.

We didn't have to wait for a decision from the Hospital Ethics Committee. We didn't have to worry about being disappointed. I didn't have to make any more train trips to the city, and I didn't have to obey strangers in dark suits.

Our fifteen-year marriage had always been a partnership. We made decisions together. But this time, David took the lead. He took charge and left our world with his dignity intact. It was his life. It was his death.

I leaned down for one last kiss. His lips were already cooling. He looked so peaceful.

The nurse waited for me to say goodbye, and then said his body would be transported to our hometown funeral parlor for cremation.

My brother-in-law, Bob, sat in the Waiting Room, ready to drive me home. He had arrived too late to say goodbye, but I encouraged him to do so anyway. Brothers can always communicate.

Then, in silence, we walked to the car in the underground parking garage. My wool coat protected me from the February night air. My flushed face repelled the chill.

I sat alone in the back seat and stared at the moon through the window. It was full and seemed to be looking straight at me. For a moment, a smile seemed to appear on the lunar surface and my mind veered away from reality. I read it as my signal that David had arrived in Heaven. He was without pain. He would be my guardian angel from now on. Suddenly, I felt a little better.

The headlights of the car illuminated the metal guard rails on the Pennsylvania Turnpike. They sped by and counted down the distance to home, and mesmerized me with the rhythm of their passing.

"I will be fine."

Bob wanted to come inside with me as support when I broke the tragic news to my children.

"Thanks, anyway, Bob, but I have to do this alone. We'll be fine."

My gloved hand turned the key in the door knob. It was late, but the children were still awake. They were watching the *Grammy Awards* with my sister, Chris, who had flown from California to be with me.

They stared at me in unison, and waited.

"I have something to tell you…" I began. *I am completely and utterly lost.*

* * *

Food for Thought
by Lauretta L. Kehoe
CWI Contest Finalist 2017

Space is a long dark thing. I have been drifting for an eternity, past planets and stars that have no life or food. Many do have elements of existence, but I cannot consume their thoughts as they are too vast for my digestion.

So, I drift…

There is a planet covered with white clouds in beautiful designs. Maybe I will find creatures limited enough to provide my needs. I crave spicy flavors. I will investigate.

I float down through a light blue sky where the clouds make a soft ceiling. Tall brown objects with a head of smaller green particles reach up to greet me. I settle on the green springy floor and permeate the outer shell of the tall brown things, but they have no thoughts, or thoughts too distant for my use. I will look elsewhere.

A small creature with transparent wings flies by. It is yellow and black and makes a pleasant humming sound. I surround its body and fill myself with its existence. I see others in a structure of many hexagonal openings. They have a need to deliver the sweet-smelling juices of multi-petaled objects to their dwelling. They gather the succulent wetness from the vivid hues together and return to their home nearby. I take my fill from the little beings. They fall down and are still. I have taken all of their thoughts, but I am not filled.

A small brown creature scurries up the side of the tall brown objects. I encompass the little thing and enter. There is more to this one than the flying things. Thoughts of gathering food and storing it, of avoiding larger, more dangerous creatures. I consume its thoughts. It stops, not knowing what it was doing. I can suckle no more so I move on.

Above me soars a blue, flying organism. Wide wings beat the air to carry it above the heads of the tall thoughtless ones. I join with it and we climb higher in the blue sky. I enjoy the sights, the sense of freedom and the strong wings. I absorb all the beauty above and below. The winged thing carries me further into this lush world, and then falls to the ground after I empty it.

There is a structure below. I feel the thoughts of many creatures. I settle into a larger being curled up, staring at a box that shows others of like manner. I fill this one's head. It calls itself "woman." There is much to feast on in this one's thoughts… emotions caused by the little box before her.

I fade into her consciousness and drink delicious morsels, savoring each one as it is produced. She is watching what she calls "the soaps." I wonder at the power of such a thing as I digest intense emotions. I nibble at the grief she feels for another who does not produce thoughts. How can that be?

I slowly ingest the appetizing anger. It has been so long since I have feasted on thoughts such as these. I will stay awhile.

The woman hears a noise. We go into another area of the structure she calls home. There is a littler one that does not look like the woman. I derive from my food source that this is a "baby." I enter the baby and am suddenly drawn into a wide world of wispy thoughts. Much more than the woman, yet of a different consistency. There are sweet thoughts, dainty thoughts, playful thoughts. They reach out to unlimited resources. I gorge myself on this dessert, immersed in the lightness of the child's imagination. I've always liked a dessert after a heavy meal like the woman's mind. I eat my fill and I am satisfied.

Much later, and I am still hungry. I settle into the woman's brain again, but a man enters the home-- the woman's mate. I move, intrigued by this new delicacy.

I penetrate his mind, taste spicy things. This is more to my liking than the heavy thoughts of the woman. I am in ecstasy as I slowly ingest the man's thoughts about another woman who does not live in this house. His body is connected to the woman. His mind burns with desire. I begin to feel light-headed and realize I am drunk on the man's passion. I prefer robust food when I can get it, and this man is a wonderful source.

I wonder that none of my people have discovered this planet's rich food source. The famine we experienced could be alleviated so quickly and enjoyably. I must remember to take samples of the resplendent crop home. I settle back, drink more and revel in my meal.

I awaken hungry, terribly hungry, but my food source is asleep. No thoughts come from their empty minds. They have closed down their bodies for the night. This is not a good thing. My people must be prepared to change their eating habits if these beings cannot make thoughts half the day. I go out searching for food in the stillness of the night.

I sense something! There, in the space behind a large empty house. I move to investigate and find a man and woman in that dark place. The man is standing over the woman with an object in his hand. The woman is lying on the ground with her outer skin removed. I can sense her fear. Juicy. I will save that for later.

I move into the man for nourishment. His thoughts are overwhelming. He is an infinite supply of food. I relish in the colorful concepts as he moves over the woman. There is hate. There is grief. There is excitement. There is play. And there is something I cannot identify. A virtual storehouse of victuals!

I gorge on his emotions, yet he seems unaffected. Here is an endless supply of food and it is all mine! The passion and hatred is enough to feed several of my kin many days. It is too much to believe. All the colors swirl about me with passionate velocity.

I gorge myself on his rage, his uncontrollable urge to consume the woman. He leaves her on the ground and we flee into the night. I will stay with him. I feast on all shades of black and violet rolling around his head in beautiful configurations. Images of past encounters flood his memories, and I indulge in his fantasies, rich with flavor. I am inebriated on his bizarre concepts. Filled to capacity. Abundant with his thoughts. Yet I crave more. I gorge and gorge and cannot stop! I am captive to his turmoil. I know I should stop. I am saturated to the point of bursting. I must stop. I cannot stop.

The man stops by another structure and watches a young woman in her room. We walk around the home and go to her. I sense her fear without even entering her mind. The man's burning desire is uncontrollable. We both drink with rage and intense hatred.

I… must… withdraw! I have eaten my fill! But something about this intellect holds me captive. It surrounds me and drinks me as I have others. I must stop. Black and violet haze grips me, illusions too grotesque for even me to comprehend. His flames feed on the fear of the women he destroys. Black smoke of nightmare apparitions envelops me.

I must warn my people! We cannot handle this overwhelming species as I first believed. We cannot handle the overload. I am locked in the man's mind, consumed by the very food I crave. I only wanted a taste of this world… only a bite.

I am completely and utterly lost.

The escaped mental patient wandered the silent town looking for something. Why was he covered with blood? Where had he been? What had he done? It was as though something had eaten his mind. The psychopath stopped in his frenzied tracks. "I'm hungry," he said to himself. "I need something to eat."

He drifted on in the quiet, deserted streets, looking for a woman to devour.

* * *

The Expeditioneer
by Lily Medlock
CWI Contest Finalist 2017

"I'll tell them you died a hero." His fist connected with her face.

Cruselle shrieked and scrambled back to her feet. She didn't want to hurt Sioned. She loved him. *He* loved *her.* At least that's what she thought. It was hard to tell now that he was standing across from her, teeth bared, fists clenched. "You don't have to do this," Cruselle said. "Please, Sioned. This isn't you!"

He jabbed at her face.

She ducked and swiped a foot across his ankles, hooking her leg behind his knee.

He toppled to the ground beside her.

Cruselle crawled tentatively to his side, slowly, carefully wrapping her arms around him and bringing her mouth to his. Willing him, pleading for him to come back to her.

He stopped fighting. For a moment they touched and everything was like before. They pulled apart. His breath tickled her neck as he whispered, "All those people waiting back home. They're going to miss you."

Her eyes flew open. "Why?" Her voice was soft.

His lips grazed hers once more. "Silly girl," the man said against Cruselle's mouth. "You didn't truly think I would let you return in one piece."

She pushed off his chest.

"No, no," he continued, making his way to his feet. "It just won't do to share the glory of finding the artifact." He circled his companion like a wild cat waiting to pounce on its next meal.

Cruselle's shirt had ridden up around her torso and she pulled it down. She looked at the man before her, such a far cry from the gentleman she had met that day. The one who had picked her up off the ground and led her toward the bright, new world. The one who had helped her through expedition training. The one who had showered her with compliments and kisses. The one who had become her closest friend.

Their meeting played over and over in her mind, a sick reminder that this sneering monster who paced the stark, white space pod was not her Sioned. She was leaning against a wall in an empty hallway, her knees pulled up against her chest. Her head rested on her crossed arms, and her body shook with sobs. She didn't want to be here. She didn't want to be an Expeditioneer and she didn't want to travel the lengths of the universe to hunt for the artifact.

She hadn't worried when she took the test. She had no interest in going into space, so she wouldn't be chosen anyway. But then the results arrived. One hundred percent compatible! Those were the words stamped across her test papers, and those words followed her everywhere.

She barely had time to process what that meant before Government officials came to her home and ripped her away to this place. Five other young men and women were also at the academy, without any pretense of explanation.

Cruselle held it together in front of the others while the leader explained they had been chosen to be Expeditioneers. They would go into space to search for the artifact that would save their nation from a never-ending war.

A uniformed guard led her to a drab room with a small bed huddled in the corner and a desk collecting dust against the opposite wall. There were no windows. Cruselle felt the walls pushing in on her, and felt the strangling silence. An overwhelming sense of panic made her run down the hall and put as much distance between her and that room as possible. Then she felt a presence, and looked up to find a pair of boot-clad feet shifting in front of her.

"Are you okay?" A handsome man stood with his hands in his pockets, looking down at her pitiful figure.

She pushed white-blond hair out of her face and

rubbed her eyes. She tried to collect herself, but the reality of the situation pressed upon her, overwhelming her once more. She clamped her eyes shut and squeezed a few more tears out. "I am completely and utterly lost," she whispered.

"Oh," the man replied. "I-I'm sorry." He paused. "I didn't necessarily appreciate being dragged here either." He turned and settled down beside her.

There was a slight accent to his words, something sweet and lilting that made Cruselle yearn to hear him go on. She managed a weak smile.

"I think it'll be alright. I really do," he said, toying with a thick lock of sandy hair. "When you stop to think about it, we could be the ones to rebuild our crumbling nation. We could save the world!"

Cruselle failed to return his enthusiasm.

The man placed a warm hand on her shoulder and patted it awkwardly. "Let's go see what's available in the kitchen, huh? There's no point being lost on an empty stomach."

She felt an odd attraction to this charming stranger. In a matter of minutes, he had managed to make her feel better. She nodded.

The man held out his hand. "I'm Sioned."

She took it gingerly. "Cruselle."

But that man couldn't possibly be the one who stood before her now.

"Darling Cruselle," Sioned drawled, stroking a finger down the countless controls of the pod's dashboard. "My plan worked out so well, you see. Befriend the Expeditioneer with the highest score, dispose of the others, then use her to get the artifact."

Cruselle pressed a hand to her mouth as his words sunk in. Abby and Isabelle, Max and Havia, they were all gone because of him.

"Of course, I'll have to kill you before I go home, so I can return to accept full responsibility for saving the nation and stopping the war. They'll praise me like a saint. I may even be knighted!"

Sioned turned back to the girl weeping on the floor. "No one will remember the girl who made a perfect score on her test. How sad, lost to a terrible accident."

He spoke so calmly. So sure of himself. Cruselle couldn't stand the creature who wore Sioned's face, and she wouldn't sit here and wait to die. Her training had taught her a few things.

Cruselle struggled to a standing position and gasped, "Sioned…" Her voice was thick around the lump in her throat. She took a few steps toward him and held out her arms as if to embrace him.

He stood there and smirked.

Cruselle savored the whoosh of his escaping breath as she charged, ramming her head into his stomach.

His eyes grew wide as he fell back against the control panel. Cruselle grabbed him by the front of the shirt and punched his face.

It didn't take long to realize he had fallen into the grav-regulation dial, because the gravity level in the pod dropped very, very low. Cruselle and Sioned drifted to the ceiling.

Her ears popped as she kept fighting.

It was slow and sloppy, but each opponent got in a few blows. The air tinted with the scent of blood and sweat. As the pod air conditioning kicked in to stir the hot air, Cruselle wiped a hand across a black eye and braced for another strike.

Then a knife appeared in Sioned's hand. "My dear, when will you learn to give up?" he drawled.

The world slowed, but Cruselle redoubled her efforts, swinging wildly, lashing out with her last bit of energy. The adrenaline had kicked in, making her moves jittery and uncontrolled.

Sioned shoved her across the room, and angled his blade. His face reflected hate, resentment, jealousy and greed.

She was lost without him, but without the artifact, the nation would be lost. The war would be lost! She had to make sure the artifact reached the right hands.

Sioned's blade glinted in the dim starlight as he adjusted his grip.

It was him or her.

Suddenly, Cruselle surged, flipping and scrambling through open air and pinning the only man she thought she could trust against the pod door. He tried to push away, but her hands were wrapped around his neck and she had swiped his long knife.

Cruselle's lovely face twisted in rage. She pulled an oxygen mask to her mouth and released Sioned, grabbing the safety rail imbedded in the ceiling.

Sioned's eyes widened and his lips pulled away from his teeth in a snarl. Cruselle slammed her hand down on the OPEN button on the control panel and squeezed her eyes shut.

A swooshing vacuum sucked Sioned into the abyss. The door shut automatically and the oxygen level returned to normal. Cruselle drifted around the cabin, opened her eyes and wrapped her arms around herself as she shuddered with every breath. Tears gathered on her lashes. She blinked them away, and they floated in front of her face.

Looking through the constellation of fat, glittering droplets, Cruselle murmured to herself, "I am completely and utterly lost."

* * *

Matilijas
by C. Lee McKenzie
CWI Contest Finalist 2017 & Judge's Pick

The July sun ran the thermometer up to ninety degrees by eleven that morning. The corn tassels drooped in the vegetable garden watered only two hours before, and Elaine's dark curls clung lifeless against her forehead. She set aside her rake and walked up the path to the road that wound past her house. The air was cooler here, but only a bit, so she leaned against the stone wall that still held some of the night chill. The leggy stems of red poppies shadowed her face.

The Matilijas, unlike the rest of the vegetation, looked fresh. Their wide open petals strained upward like true sun worshipers, unafraid and trusting.

Elaine acknowledged their bravery and resented it at the same time. How she yearned to trade the pinched feeling inside her for such openness and faith. Yet turning her face skyward in this heat was out of the question. Besides, no amount of sun would brighten the dark space surrounding her heart. She slid down the wall and sat in the shade of the poppies, her long legs pulled tight against her chest.

Between eleven and noon in the summer, Elaine always sat next to the rock wall, under the comfort of the Matilijas. She sought shelter there in the winter as well, when the Matilijas had been cut to stubble and sulked underground, waiting for their next season.

Winter waiting was the most difficult for Elaine. With no Matilijas to see or touch, she had to draw on her memory of their gold centers and floppy white perimeters. She had to hold on to her belief that they would return in June.

"If they don't, I am completely and utterly lost. Again."

The mail delivery came at the same time each weekday. Elaine depended on the time as much as she depended on the snub-nosed blue and white truck to bring her messages from other places.

Every day she acknowledged that what she did now and had done for over a year was not really living. Since the accident, she'd not worked, not met her friends, not left this place that tucked snuggly against the California mountainside, for more than groceries in town. She'd become a rooted thing clinging to the earth around her. She must. In this place she could be somewhat safe, at times centered, and on good days, free to pretend the way they all used to, together.

"You remember, don't you?" she said to the poppies. "Those other summers when the asphalt heated to a shimmer, and all of us sat in this very spot?

Sometimes she and her girls became bandits or shivered, hiding from kidnappers, not daring to breathe as the evildoers crept past their secret place among the poppies.

Elaine brushed the tiny beads of perspiration from her forehead. On truly hot days like this, they'd sip lemonade and make faces because Elaine refused to put too much sugar in the mix.

"Not good for your teeth, darlings!" Her words came back to her from that other time. Before. The girls sitting beside her sipped the tangy juice and scrunched their faces and laughed. The Matilijas shook overhead from the laughing and the bitter-lemon shuddering.

"Stop it, you two. Don't make such faces. They'll freeze like that and you'll both be terrible sights forever." Her stern voice was such fraud.

They didn't believe her, of course, and scrunched up their noses even more. Then they'd play another game because it was hot and summer, and in the shade of the Matilijas, any game was the best.

Elaine's memories stabbed at her, and she jerked away from the wall to stop them from tunneling through her like hungry shrews.

Had the truck left the post office yet, she wondered? *Was it driving up the mountain to where she waited? Was it past noon?* The yellow and white poppy faces nodded in a draft that vanished before it became a true breeze.

Sometimes the girls pretended an ambush. That was a game that delighted them more than anything. The *ambushee*, usually their quite-suspecting dad, played his part so well that they would console and kiss and hug him to make sure he recovered from the shock of their attack.

Elaine adored the game, too. After an especially successful ambush, she served cookies to the victim and the Gang-of-Two.

They sat together on the deck and told about the day. They talked of the heat, the dinner to come. She treasured that time. After the games. Before dinner and bed and stories. Then later, she nestled against Peter while the house settled into night, and together they listened to the girls' sleepy sounds in the next room.

Now Elaine had difficulty deciding which of these parts of her day were her favorite. They each vied for first place.

The Matilijas nodded and their shadows trembled around her like small ghosts. She missed Peter most in the afternoon and at night, of course. The lanky curve of her body had fit perfectly into his long, lean frame. When he had held her, her dark and untamable hair fell across the pale skin of his arm.

Opposites that suited each other.

The girls she missed always. But in the mornings, especially between eleven and noon all summer, her loneliness gnawed at her like a canker. It roamed freely inside her all day and into the night until she slept. But then there were the dreams, and so sleep gave no relief.

"Was that the truck?" She pulled the leaves apart and peered down the road. But there was nothing. A little longer. She had to wait... to be patient.

The girls were never patient. Birthdays, Christmas, a trip to the store or the beach--all impatient times. Marie, the eldest with her father's dark eyes, never waited for the surprise. She always ferreted out the hidden cake, the tucked-away presents. Kara was quick to learn her sister's skills. Peter used to say, "They must be part bloodhound."

"I should have put more sugar in the lemonade." Elaine spoke to the nearest Matilija, and pressed her fingertips against her temples. Her head ached as memories played in her mind.

Peter let them have anything they wanted.

Her mother said he spoiled them.

Elaine agreed, but excused him. "He loves them, Mom."

"But, Elaine, Peter has to learn when to say no to those two. Otherwise they'll grow up to be terrible people. Greedy and full of me, me, me! You don't want that, do you?"

"No, of course not, Mom. But I can't tell him how to rear his girls."

"If you don't, who will?"

How many times did this conversation happen? And why was it still so clear?

In the end, she decided her mom was right. She would tell Peter he had to stop spoiling his daughters, but whenever she was about to, she couldn't. Finally, she decided she'd let him spoil them, but she would not. She'd punish. She'd say, no. She'd make them brush their teeth after meals. She'd pass on the virtues her parents had taught her.

"You should be saving some of your allowance for the future. You know, for college. Budget yourselves today, so you won't have to worry later."

Her advice was so like her mother's. She had to be telling them the right things. She shook her head at herself now. What did second and third graders know about college or budgets? What did she know about advice?

Elaine remembered that last morning so clearly.

Peter waiting in the car outside, not so subtly tapping impatiently on the steering wheel. The girls submitting to one last hair brushing, gobbling their toast, and gathering scattered homework papers. Late again for school if they didn't hurry. Each begging for a short-term loan from Banker Mom. But she held fast. She wouldn't spoil them. Besides, Peter would give them each two dollars on the trip to school. She waved them off. Peter raced to end of the road and at the corner whipped his wheels into a sharp left.

"Be careful," she muttered to herself. "Don't drive so fast." Then as if it were any other morning, she went back inside to stack the dishes in the dishwasher and to dress for work. She'd also be late if she didn't hurry.

The sound of the mail truck coming down the road, froze Elaine's memory at the moment she picked up her keys and the phone rang.

"Thank you," she whispered, grateful for the mailman's punctuality. She depended on it to freeze her at that precious second. At the door, gripping the keys. A tiny drop of time suspended above a still pond. The last moment of her life. Before.

The mailman flipped down the metal door and tossed the letters inside. With a flick of a wrist, he closed the door, and in seconds, drove away.

But Elaine didn't move from under the poppies. She didn't want to rush to the box and find only the mail order catalogues or bills. Or yet another letter from her mother, pleading. "If you won't come to me, let me come to you."

She'd wait here a little longer. It was time to think of another game to play. A game she could play by herself under the Matilijas that, like her, would abide in this place season after season.

* * *

About Time
by Tomas Marcantonio
CWI Contest Finalist 2017

The line of food tents along the roadside smoked, their lanterns swinging over plates of fire-red kimchi, and shot glasses filled to the brim with sour-smelling soju.

Green neon signs glowed on Christina's thinning curls and gave her sallow cheeks a new menace as she wielded the fish knife.

A squatty foreigner with a toad-like face pulled her own knife and faced the Brit, barking something shocking in Korean.

Christina responded with cold, distant eyes, determined to keep her seat and continue drinking until she forgot her aged loneliness.

"For goodness sake!" Maggie said. "If she wants our seat, let her have it. We've finished eating."

"I haven't finished by a long chalk," Christina snapped, brandishing the knife with arthritic fingers.

Customers watched the two foreigners confront one another, fried noodles hanging from their chopsticks and mouths open in various stages of bafflement and delight.

"Put the knife down," Maggie said, her pudding cheeks flushed from the unwanted stares.

Christina shook her head stubbornly and bared her teeth like an affronted mother protecting her cubs. She growled at the elderly tent-owner who shouted at her and dropped the knife into an empty plate where it clattered, knocking chopsticks and side-dishes to the floor.

"Come on!" Christina shouted to the woman. "Take my seat if you're that desperate, but don't think for one minute I'm afraid of you!"

Maggie placed a chubby hand on her forehead in embarrassment, scooped up her handbag with the other, and then muddled off after her cousin while the tent-owner fired insults at their departing backs. "I've never been so embarrassed in my life," she said. "You saw all those people waiting to sit down. I don't know why you insisted on arguing with them."

Christina simply laughed, her anger evaporating into the warm evening air of the backstreets. "Oh, it's all good fun," she countered, stumbling a little from both drink and age. "You think all Asians are sweet and smiley, but these Koreans are tough. Good-hearted, but really tough. That last one was a fierce old bird, wasn't she? I have more respect for her than all the meek old ladies who warm themselves by their fires back in England."

Christina led them through the thronging maze of back-alleys that seemed to Maggie to spread like veins across the heart of the city. Smoke charged out into the alleyway from the open windows of bustling restaurants, carrying with it the intoxicating aromas of burning pork belly and unfamiliar spices. Tables were busy with green bottles and shot glasses, and young weekend warriors gesticulating with chopstick hands.

"Three years, and I still get lost here," Christina professed. "Isn't it wonderful?"

Maggie sidestepped into a doorway as a pack of mascara-clad, short-skirted Korean girls paraded past arm-in-arm, high-heels cutting through the smoke.

"Down here," Christina said, pointing to another row of tents tucked away down a side-street. "You get more culture in an hour at these tents than you get in a week of temple visits."

Christina greeted the tent owner in Korean and took a seat on the bench in front of the counter of meat and fish and vegetables and the grills where chicken gizzard was already smoking for other customers. Maggie squeezed her considerable frame onto the bench across from Christina while the latter ordered plates of spicy chicken, mackerel and a bottle of soju.

"Your Korean's very good," the man on the other side of Christina said. He was clean-shaven and young. The girl on his arm nodded.

"She's living here illegally," Maggie said with disapproval. "Came here on a tourist visa years ago and decided to stay."

Christina laughed. "And no one's going to find me," she said, winking at the couple and opening the bottle of soju off the counter. She poured out the clear liquid that smelled to Maggie like paint-stripper, and the couple raised their shot glasses for a toast.

"And what about you?" the young man said to Maggie. "Why did you come to Busan?"

"She had nothing better to do," Christina answered for her, laughing.

"Just visiting," Maggie said, her face still rearranging itself after the burning shock of the soju.

"She's had nothing better to do for years," Christina went on. "But there are signs she might be waking up."

The young couple smiled as Maggie shook her head and accepted a fresh glass. Their mackerel was already sizzling away over coals behind the tent. Maggie arched her neck upward to observe the blinking neon parade across the street, signs blaring pink and blue in an alien alphabet, the music seeping through the windows loud and young.

"We really must have some wine," Christina shouted to those in the tent. "When the food's done, what say we have some wine and find somewhere to dance?"

Maggie sighed and shot Christina down with

round wet eyes that reminded Christina of an evening cow that has seen its best days. Maggie rolled her eyes and turned to the couple for entertainment. "So, when are you two going to get married?" she said.

They both laughed. "We're only twenty-two," the girl said.

"Don't let the opportunity pass," Christina said. "You'll regret it if you do, and you can mark my words on that." She pointed a bony finger at the young man, and he laughed again and conceded. "But be careful. Marriage can also hold you back, like chains on a wild elephant."

"Oh, honestly," Maggie said with a frown.

"Yes," Christina said, "and it shouldn't take your husband dying for you to start living." She burped loudly after the closing remark and took another shot of soju without waiting for a toast.

Maggie shook her head and pictured her husband's face. She could see two faces now. One, the laughing, bearded giant with smile lines etched into his forehead. The other, cold, pale and empty, lying in a hospital bed.

"I'm sorry," the young man said.

Maggie shook her head.

"It's been three years," Christina said.

"Four," Maggie corrected.

"And this is the first bit of fun she's had since,

would you believe it? Sixty-eight years old and she's hardly lived a day of it."

Maggie seethed quietly while plates of fish and chicken appeared on the counter in front of them and Christina filled their glasses yet again.

"Let's go back to the first tent when we're done," Christina said suddenly, finishing her glass and reaching again for the bottle. "I wanna see that old ogre again and finish what I started."

Hours later, the twin beds were hard, and Christina's face matched while the music blared from the karaoke rooms in the next building. She lay on one bed with her sharp chin aimed at the ceiling, and wine eyes staring at nothing.

"You really must stop carrying on like this," Maggie said, folding her clothes on the bed.

"I can carry on how I want," Christina said. "At seventy-six, I've earned the right."

Maggie exhaled slowly, watching her cousin's chest rise and fall. It was their third night at the hotel and each night had ended in wine and arguments.

"You care too much what people think," Christina said, her eyes now closed.

"And you care too little," Maggie said. Maggie's bulky body caved the bed as she sat on the side thinking of the many uncomfortable nights ahead and the two faces of her husband. "I suppose you're planning on more of the same tomorrow," she said with a tired voice.

"Stop supposing," Christina snapped. "You have too many worries. Too many worries and too many chins." She kept her eyes closed to stop the room from spinning. She would never get anywhere with this dry balloon she called a cousin. Her companion was far too careful and not nearly enough fun. Christina knew very few people would attend her own funeral, but at least people would say she had travelled, she had guts and she had wine. She thought of the man she left at the altar fifty years ago. If only she'd had guts in those days.

"Just think," Christina said. "If I had gone through with the wedding, it might have been you living here alone, and *me* wasting away with that bearded fool."

"He wasn't a fool," Maggie said quietly.

"He was," Christina insisted, her eyebrows raised but eyes still closed. "But he was a fine fool, and he would have made me very happy if only I'd gone through with it."

Maggie looked softly on the deteriorating face of her cousin. Even with her eyes closed, Maggie could still see the young woman with long silky hair and sharp eyes that stopped men in their tracks.

"You were good for him, you know," Christina

went on, her words slow and fading now. "And he was good for you, too. But it's about time to spread those wings and jump." Christina sank into sleep thinking of the crushed face of the bearded man at the altar and her own quiet funeral.

Maggie continued to watch the slow breathing of her cousin and the half-drunk glass of red on Christina's bedside table. *Travelling is for skinny people and drunks,* Maggie thought. She turned the light off and thought of the past three nights--the fights, the strangers, the new smells and flavours and long nights in back-alleys. The anxiety of coming days and nights made her heart race. She thought of the past four years. Nights spent alone. Wasted. Looking at photos of the bearded giant she had loved. She looked out at the flashing indecipherable lights and the circuit board of winding alleys that disappeared into the night.

"I am completely and utterly lost," she said to herself. She turned toward the sleeping silhouette of her cousin. "And maybe you're right. Maybe it's about time."

* * *

Nan's Spirit
by J. Lenni Dorner
CWI Contest Finalist 2017

I make my final tweak to the time machine chamber. The elevator opens and Musheera, carrying two silver protection suits, steps out.

"Glad that's finally working. One hundred fifty meters of stairs were killing me."

We help each other into the suits. I'm careful of Musheera's hijab. It got stuck in the zipper of her previous protection suit. She wept for an hour as I cut the expensive fabric to free her.

"Your mind needs to be on the task, Spirit," she scolds.

"Of course. You're right." After a deep breath, I press the bright green button. All the instruments and panels in the room light up. "I will save my beloved."

"My cousin is lucky to have you. Go, find a cure, and I will see you in the blink of an eye," Musheera says. "Peace be upon you."

I climb into the time machine chamber. *What if no one speaks a language I know? What if there are no people?* Fear and doubt creep in. But my reason for going far outweighs every counter argument.

Musheera seals the chamber and goes to the

control panel. I watch her flick the switches and press the buttons. She focuses on the viewing monitor while pressing the final one.

The journey lasts for three successive hiccups. Strong hiccups, each causing me to wince, but then it's done. My body rematerializes in total darkness. And then I fall. The floor of the chamber is gone! Pain rockets through me as I crash into rocks that trap my left hand and crush the bones. Warm blood runs down my sleeve. I struggle, hanging by my trapped hand. The glove of my suit rips. More blood spills out, making my crushed hand slippery. Rocks pelt my protection suit as I break free. But to what end? I half slide, half tumble down a long, dark shaft.

I land on my wounded left hand. Another shockwave of pain shoots through me. A dim light clicks on overhead, revealing a stunt-airbag under me.

"Hello," a beautiful voice says.

It takes a moment to focus my tear-filled eyes.

A woman kneels beside me. Her soft hand clamps over my wound.

The pain vanishes. "How'd you do that?"

She smiles.

"I am completely and utterly lost. Where and when am I?"

The woman's head tilts to her shoulder twice, as if she's cracking her neck. "You are Spirit Medina.

Approximately three hundred of your years ago, you used the Medina-Chaudhuri time machine. The chamber is seventy meters above us."

I nod. The dim light increases in brightness at a comfortable pace. I access my injuries. "My hand!" I attempt to pull away from her, but her grip is too strong. "My suit is compromised. I could infect you with any number of diseases from my time, and vice versa."

"Do not be afraid, Spirit. I am Nan. I am without disease."

A tear rolls from my right eye. "Without disease? I have traveled far enough into the future to find cures?"

"Please." Nan releases me and motions to a door, or at least something like a door. It's a blue drawing on a white wall. The handle does not protrude.

"How do I open this?" My left hand touches the knob drawing. Though I'm not sure why it should work, I feel cool metal and am able to turn it.

"My hand is back." I flex my fingers. Other than the ripped off glove, it's as good as new. Even the blood has been cleaned away.

"Nan heals," the woman says as she walks by. More drawn-doors appear as I stare at the walls. A modified golf cart waits in a well-lit hallway. "You are familiar with this type of vehicle. It was chosen from your time as the easiest to recreate and alter. Please sit."

I sit in the passenger seat and Nan speeds the cart down the hall, far faster than fifteen miles an hour. The lighting grows dimmer as the cart surges around a bend. "Don't suppose seatbelts were part of the alteration?"

Nan tilts her head for a moment. "No. Seatbelts were only made prior to Lost Hope."

I cling to my seat. "What's Lost Hope?"

Again, Nan tilts and then straightens her head. Her mouth opens wide, as if she's anticipating a dental examination. A recording plays through her.

"Humanity is completely and utterly lost. Those who survived the first three waves of nuclear detonation will soon die from radiation or starvation. This is," static cuts into the recording, "Lost Hope." Her jaw clicks as her mouth closes.

"That was the voice of the President's oldest son, from my time. Nuclear detonation? You aren't human?" My stomach twists. It's a lot to take in. Then again, when I left, war seemed inevitable.

"I am Nan."

"Are you a robot? An Android?" I poke her arm. There's a fleshy, springy response. "You're so lifelike."

"I am Nan."

"What's a Nan?" I wonder if machines are all

that remain.

Nan blinks. "I am Nan. No head injury was registered. Are you experiencing an abnormality?"

"If you aren't human, what are you? Where did you come from? How did you come to exist?"

"I am as human as everyone else in Found. I live in Found, as everyone does since Lost Hope."

I've always hated talking to machines. "Where, or what, is Found?"

We've been driving for a long time. The hallway has a dim yellow or green light every so often.

Nan tilts her head. "Found is the only place left. It was built by Chaudhuri's chosen. The initial underground location existed primarily to preserve and protect the Medina-Chaudhuri time machine. To keep the space viable, it became the location of Project Equality."

"What's that?"

Nan's head tilts only slightly this time. "Project Equality began before Lost Hope. They selected fifty infants and twenty adults. The purpose of Project Equality was to determine if hatred could be removed from humanity. War, murder, rape, incest, torture, violent demonstrations that prohibited the free exercise of religious worshipping, dishonor among families and communities, theft, vandalism, and other such problems had infected the population and governing bodies."

"Sounds familiar," I said, recalling the egging I received and chants of, "Go back to Mexico." The protestors didn't care that I, my parents and also grandparents were born in America. Hatred is blind to truth.

"Musheera and I discussed creating such a social experiment, but the funding was never there."

"She received her inheritance after you left."

"Ah," I nod.

"Project Equality was far enough below ground that, when the nuclear waves hit, the seventy people remained unharmed. They were never meant to be the last of humanity. If the time chamber hadn't been so deep, the Project base wouldn't have survived. All would have perished."

Nan turns the cart as the hallway splits. "When the population outgrew the first location, the people dug deeper. This is the main passage tunnel. It was maintained for your arrival."

Nan adjusts the steering wheel again. The hallway lights are blue now, spaced closer together, and getting brighter.

"The current settlement is called Found. It is in a modified cavern."

"And that's where we're going?"

"Yes. Everyone is eager to meet you.

Calculating when you would arrive, converting your years to ours, and determining where you would appear has been a top priority since the beginning."

I whistle, long and slow. "Why do you say 'my years' as if we have different definitions? And why was it hard to know where I would appear? The time machine chamber was stationary."

"During Lost Hope, possibly after the destruction of the moon, Earth shifted. As the sky is no longer visible, it is difficult to determine our exact position. We dug a new chamber to receive you. It was mostly accurate." Nan taps my left hand.

We stop at a wall. A drawing of a door appears, and Nan leads the way.

At least five hundred people surround a stone platform and they cheer as we enter.

"Welcome!" A woman wearing brown crosses the platform. She bows her covered head before turning to the crowd. "Blessings upon us all! Nan, our wisest elder, has brought Spirit Medina at last."

The crowd cheers. People rush the platform. They hug me, shake my hands, and kiss my cheeks. It's hard to breathe in this mob of love.

Drums sound. The crowd disperses, some to a dancing area, others to a separate chamber in the well-lit cavern. The woman in brown escorts us.

"I am Lime, the oldest of Generation Three," she

says. "Will you join me at this table?" The table is a flat stone balanced on stalagmites, encircled with cushioned chairs.

"Thank you. Generation Three. Which generation held the fifty infants?" The table of food and drink makes me realize how empty my stomach is.

"Please, help yourself. All that is belongs to all who are," Lime says as she takes a slice of bread. "The fifty were Generation One, of which Nan is the only remaining one."

I nearly spit out my drink. "You're over three centuries old? How is that possible?"

Nan looks away.

Lime answers me. "After your departure, Musheera Chaudhuri created Project Equality. Half of the twenty adults were leaders in medicine. The purpose of the time travel was, after all, to find a cure for the disease of your spouse. Musheera wanted you to know she did not give up on that, even if it was pointless."

"Pointless?" The world gets too dark, and my body gets too heavy.

"Angel, your spouse, had gone to the medical place." Lime pulls out a clear screen. Words appear, then images. "Angel gave genetic material. The two of you were using a..." She squints and looks to Nan.

"Surrogate. They called them surrogates. It is a

word from before nanite hybrids. A living human used like our panpods." Nan said.

Lime shudders.

"Yes. In case we couldn't find the cure. Or in case I was unable to return. We wanted a child."

Lime taps the screen. "Angel was in a fatal car accident on the way home. Due to the disease, and the limitations of medicine at that time, survival was impossible."

I put my head down and wept. "Time travel was cheaper and easier to come up with than a cure. I have to go back! Now that I know the machine works, I can send Angel here. It isn't pointless, and it isn't too late in my time."

Lime frowns. "Angel died three minutes before you left. As you cannot travel before that point, altering that fate is impossible. I'm sorry."

Nan takes my hand. "I don't know if it will ease your pain, but I was born. Because of the will you and Angel left, Musheera became my guardian. She protected me and your machine. If not for that, she would not have funded Project Equality. And it wouldn't have been located where it was. Spirit, it is because of your influence and the choices you and Angel made that we have survived."

I nod. Then Nan whispers in my ear, "I am your daughter. My name was once Sky Medina."

"What? The surrogacy worked? Our odds were so low!" For the first time, I look at Nan. Really look. She has Angel's nose and my chin. How did I not see that?

"Why did you change your name to Nan?"

She looks away.

Lime turns the screen off. "Grandmother started calling herself Nan after the nanite hybrids had covered ninety percent of her body."

I touch my daughter's chin so she'll look at me again. "You aren't nanites. You are a human. You are my Sky."

* * *

Scattered Debris
by Jaimi-Lynn Smith
CWI Contest Finalist 2017

The spring heat bore down through the shade of the thin, cream-colored canopy. Leah loved it when bluebonnets dotted the Texas country hills. She studied their dancing, wishing fervently that Jordan could watch them sway with her. The bluebonnets were his favorite and the two always walked among them during the season.

She swiveled to face forward in her chair, feeling a bit disoriented. The man before her was speaking, though she couldn't register what he was saying. A shredded tissue sat in her lap, pieces of it leaving debris across the smooth skirt of her satin black dress. Unsure of how it got there, she picked it up and twisted it in her hands, shredding it further. A bluebird flew in the distance and she locked eyes on its wings, once again blocking out the words of the man in front of her.

Her best friend, Ava, laid a gentle hand on hers, snapping her back to attention. "It's time," she said quietly, her tender voice nudging Leah to stand. She pressed a single red rose into Leah's hand and guided her forward, toward the man that had finally quit speaking.

A smooth, dark wooden coffin lay closed, ready to be lowered into the ground.

Leah ran a clammy hand over the cool, polished wood and felt a quick, shivering panic rise within her. The coffin held her husband, Jordan, and the hand on the coffin trembled when she pictured waking up tomorrow without him.

"I can't do this," Leah whispered, voice breaking. Her eyes brimmed in terror when she turned to Ava. Her gaze strayed again to the window and the bluebonnets. She wouldn't hold his hand and walk through them this year. *I'm a widow,* she thought. *I'm not ready for that title.* The first tear escaped, blurring her vision of the pretty blossoms.

Her aunt rushed forward to join Ava, blocking Leah from the view of the others in attendance. Her aunt spoke low, but strong, as she leveled her eyes to meet Leah's. "Sweetie, you can do this. Just place the rose on the casket and this part is over."

Leah shook her head as another tear fell. She blinked rapidly and moved her vision past her aunt's shoulder to the crowd of people. Jordan hated spectacles and the idea that she may make one at an event in his honor had her spine snapping straight. A numbness settled over her, stemming the tears.

She took a breath and turned back to the cold,

shiny coffin. Once again, she rested her hand on its smooth surface and felt a jolt of pain as Jordan's bright, sweet smile flashed into her mind. She laid the rose delicately on the casket as unbearable pain blossomed through her being. She would never see that smile or hold his hand again. She would never smell his skin or hear his voice. The pain was burning out the numbness as the shaking through her body increased. She turned from the coffin and dropped back into her seat, silent tears streaming onto a dress still blotted with forgotten lint from a tattered tissue.

There was already a smattering of people in her home when Ava helped Leah from the car. Her entire body ached with grief, and she wanted nothing more than to crawl into bed and shut the world out. Her emotions felt paralyzed, but when she walked into the sea of sympathy filling the home she and Jordan had built together, a touch of resentment sneaked beneath the paralysis. She tried to suppress it and graciously accept hugs and condolences, but by the time she sank into the soft leather of her living room sofa, she was exhausted and irritable.

Ava slipped a glass of deep red wine into her hand. "Take a few sips, best friend. It will help."

Leah blindly followed instructions, breathing in the familiar scent of her favorite Cabernet before taking three swift sips. Though Jordan didn't drink, he built Leah a beautiful wine cabinet fully stocked with all her favorites. *He was such a thoughtful man.* Anger pierced her heart as she swirled her glass. *Well, he was usually thoughtful.*

She felt the couch dip slightly as someone sat beside her. She peered over her wine glass and into the clear, whiskey brown eyes of her aunt.

Her aunt smoothly took the half empty glass from her hand and replaced it with a plate of food.

The sight of food was revolting, and she said as much before her aunt pinned her with those bright eyes.

"Leah Danielle, you need to eat." The use of her full name brought a ghost of a smile to her lips. Since her mother passed, her aunt had been her friend and mentor, and she only used both names when Leah was being severely stubborn.

She studied the plate and sighed heavily. "Why did you only bring casseroles?" She pushed her food across the plate with the fork.

"Sweetie, it's a funeral in the South, and there are *only* casseroles." She tucked a stray strand of Leah's light brunette hair behind the delicate shell of her ear. "Try the chicken. You'll like it."

She said it in such a way that Leah knew she had no choice. Resigned, Leah nodded and sampled the chicken. It didn't taste like ashes, so she donated a slight smile and sampled a second bite. After she broke off a piece of roll and managed to swallow it, her aunt handed her the wine.

"Good girls get treats," she said, patting Leah's knee.

Leah gulped the remainder of the wine before finishing the roll.

Picking up the empty wine glass, her aunt gave Leah's knee a final pat. "This is a battle you must face, and nothing I can say will make it easier. You'll survive this. You're a strong girl."

For the next two hours, Leah stayed seated, slowly sipping the fresh glass of wine that someone, probably Ava, had slipped into her hand. She nibbled as a constant wave of family and friends slid beside her to offer prayers and condolences. By the time the crowd faded from her home, a tingle of madness crawled into her brain, and she found it increasingly difficult to hold onto control.

By the time the steady hum turned to a hush, only Ava remained.

Leah rose and picked her way to the kitchen where Ava worked clearing dishes. The elegant, hand-crafted kitchen island sat covered with plants and flowers from the funeral home. Leah set her wine glass aside as she noted specs of potting soil that dusted the island surface. She and Jordan had designed and built the beautiful unique island together and, in that moment, she felt a driving compulsion to see it gleam. Leah grabbed the plants and placed them haphazardly on the tiled floor.

Rushing to her aid, Ava removed the few remaining plants and handed her a cleaning cloth to buff the top.

Finally, satisfied and emotionally spent, Ava led Leah to the bedroom.

"Here, let me help you out of your dress," Ava said. "Here are some soft blue pajamas."

A tear trickled free as Leah looked around, and then more tears as every section of the room brought fresh memories to assault her. The dam erupted when she imagined Jordan standing in his pajama bottoms, bathed in the morning sun. She twisted from that vision to the leather lounge chair and saw him sprawled with his laptop, bare feet propped up as he researched a new project. Frantic, she spun and nearly fell into the large sleigh bed.

She wailed as she longed for his passionate embrace and lover's tangle in the cool grey sheets. She would never feel his teeth lightly nip her neck again. Never taste his lips pressed against hers. The aroma of his aftershave haunted the room. Anxiety and grief rained through her like a storm.

She felt the sensation of his touch as she ripped

the sheets off the bed and heaved them across the room. She pushed the mattress off the platform but could still see his sleepy smirk and hear his husky whisper of *Good morning, beautiful*. Her hair felt the tug of his hands and her tongue savored him.

"God," she wailed as she crumpled to the floor. Her voice was a study in pain as cries wracked her body.

Ava tried to comfort her friend and shed tears with her, but Leah didn't notice. Overwhelming grief swallowed her as she sobbed until her voice went hoarse. Sobbed until she felt sick. Sobbed until she collapsed from exhaustion and fell into a deep, dreamless sleep.

Despite the advice of doctor and friends, Leah went back to work in three weeks. Everything in her new world felt strangely different and she prayed a normal routine would shake the confusion that lingered. Instead, she felt coworkers cast sympathetic glances and simple tasks seemed perplexing. Drowning in sorrow and self-doubt, she grew weary of caring.

It was a stormy Saturday when Ava arrived and found Leah sitting on the sofa in the same position as the night of the funeral, holding a full glass of wine in one hand and a gun in the other. Ava, concerned, rushed to her friend.

"Leah? What are you doing?"

Leah looked at Ava with eyes rimmed red from crying. "I am completely and utterly lost, Ava." Her voice eerily reflected the statement. How could she convey the sheer disjointedness she felt? The center of her life was gone, and her existence tossed in turmoil.

"This isn't the way, Leah."

The widow's eyes snapped, a sizzle of anger in their depths. "Why? Isn't this the gun *he* used?" They hadn't talked about it. No one had, but the truth was he hadn't loved her enough to live. Something in this world made him so unhappy that he chose to escape without telling her why. Without that answer, how could she move on? She was truly and utterly lost.

"What about me Leah?" Ava said.

Leah sat blinking at the question.

"We've been best friends for decades... *decades*. I'd be lost without you. I love you, Leah. Don't do to me what he did to you."

As Leah looked down at the gun, her hand trembled and her head clouded with uncertainty. "I don't know what to do." Her voice was weak and weary. She thought of Jordan using the weapon and she felt her stomach sicken. She dropped the gun and Ava pounced, removing it from the room before taking her friend into her arms.

"We'll figure this out, best friend. We've made

it this far," Ava said as she surveyed the room. "Let's get some fresh air." She put her arm around Leah's waist and helped her through the front door. "Look," Ava said. "It's a lovely day, and the clouds are starting to clear."

* * *

Early Days
by Caroline Mansour
CWI Contest Finalist 2017

The *thwack* of the newspaper hitting the front door woke Sarah early on Saturday morning. She lay still with her eyes closed, getting her bearings, still unaccustomed to her surroundings. She breathed in the clammy air, wrinkling her nose at the sour tang wafting from her new husband's skin. Beer and cigarette smoke. A Saturday morning kind of smell, and that familiarity pushed aside the dull throb of homesickness that seemed to be her most faithful companion.

She squinted at the clock showing six a.m. and swung her legs over the side of the bed, wriggling her feet into her moccasins. She'd go for a run and try to shake off the stale remnants of the night before. Her eyes swept over Pete's sleeping form. She'd let him sleep off the hangover and then they'd do something together. She didn't know what. She'd only been in this new city two weeks, but the honeymoon glow was already beginning to fade. There must be something interesting in Cleveland.

Sarah jogged through the empty streets, committing the twists and turns of the neighborhood to memory. Her feet slapped the uneven pavement as the sky darkened, inking out its haze, whispering to leaves that hung despondently from branches. There'd be rain for sure, maybe a good thunderstorm, and she was glad she went jogging before the weather turned. With quickening pace, brisk steps cleared the echoes of last night's raucous laughter.

They'd met Pete's old friends last night at a haunt from their high school days. They were a motley group of men-boys, eager to meet "Pete's girl."

Pete glowed when he introduced his new bride and she had smiled, deeply touched by his pride. They were nice, but not much of a place for her in that crowd. Still, she was glad she'd met them. They clearly adored Pete and were thrilled to have him home.

Home. The word made her stomach flutter. This was Pete's home, not hers, but she'd be expected to make it her own.

Pete was fresh out of law school, and an incredible opportunity arose in a law firm run by his father's friend. Actually, they offered the job several months before the wedding.

Sarah couldn't shake the nagging feeling that someone had pulled the old bait and switch.

Not Pete, certainly. He was straightforward. His father, perhaps? His mother? Maybe staking her claim? The timing was certainly interesting.

Sarah pushed harder, as though she could outpace the pangs in her heart.

Home would always mean Connecticut. Her entire family lived within six miles of one another. Mom, Dad, three crazy older brothers, their wives and children, and her sweet younger sister, Cara. One big, loud, wonderful family.

She shook her head and focused again on her surroundings. She vaguely remembered a coffee shop up ahead. She would take some coffee to Pete. They would read the paper and figure out their day together. The thought cheered her immensely, even as it began to rain.

Coming out of the misty drizzle into their rental Tudor-style home, the gloom of the day crept in with her, illuminating the dingy corners and mismatched furniture she had so carefully arranged. She went around the room, turning on lamps to ward off the melancholy.

"Pete?" she called. "You up yet?"

"In the bedroom, babe."

She smiled and joined him in bed while the coffee cooled and grew stale, forgotten.

Later, she sat on their worn plaid couch playing absently with the beige vertical blinds that shaded dingy windows. *The Plain Dealer* sat unopened on the couch, reminding her that she needed to order delivery of the New York. She considered calling Cara, but decided against it. She didn't have anything new to discuss.

"I should really wash these windows," she said to Pete, who stared at the TV screen, his hands twitching as they worked on the joystick of a video game.

"What's that, sweetheart?" He responded a half minute later.

Ugh! He was like a kid when he played video games. Her brothers were the same.

"What should we do today?" she yawned, stretching languidly.

"This works for me!" he grinned, still glued to the TV screen.

She watched him for a moment. "Do you want to head downtown in a little while? Maybe have lunch and kick around? I'd like to see more of the city."

Silence.

"Pete, you're not even listening to me."

"Uh, not so much."

She stood next to him. "Come on. I'm not going to sit and watch you play video games all day."

"You don't have to watch me. Do something on your own."

"Like what? I don't even know where the

nearest mall is."

He sighed. "Maybe in a little while, okay? It's Saturday! Can we just relax for a bit?"

Sarah wandered into the kitchen. *All I do is relax.* She grimaced as the floor, a reddish Mexican tile that pulled at her feet with cold stickiness. She moved the portable dishwasher aside and grabbed a plate to make a sandwich. *Even the plates are depressing*, she thought, inspecting the floral pattern of the garage sale dishes her mother-in-law gave them last week.

The phone rang, and she heard Pete speaking. She pulled bread and mustard out of the refrigerator, folded turkey onto the bread and cut the sandwich into two triangles, like Dad always did. "It just makes it a little fancier!" he would say with a flourish. It brought a smile to her face.

"Hey!" Pete startled her. He was standing in the doorway, arms extended casually over his head, holding onto the doorframe. "So, that was Pat on the phone. He has to deliver something to Youngstown for his dad. Mind if I take a ride with him?"

She turned in disbelief, plate in hand. "Are you kidding me? I just asked you to do something with me five minutes ago and you were too busy with your video game."

"Relax, Sarah. It's not a big deal. I'm just

running an errand with him." He threw his hands up in defense.

It was too much. In one crisp motion, she smashed the plate and sandwich into the sink. "You can be so utterly insensitive, Pete. I have been in this city, *your* city, for two weeks. Jobless. Friendless. And you're going to abandon me on a Saturday to hang out with your buddy? We spent all of last night with your friends. Are you a teenager again?"

He winced, his face pale and blank.

"All I wanted was to drive downtown and get out of the neighborhood your *mother* picked out for us, and you flattened me. So go! Have a great time. I'll be here when you get back, because I always am."

He stared at her, mouth ajar, as if he were about to say something, then left the room.

She heard the door latch click, and all was quiet. Sarah crumpled into a kitchen chair, laid her cheek on the table and wept. Not just at the silly fight, although she was already beginning to regret her explosion. She sobbed at the strain of the wedding and leaving home and the deep and wretched loneliness that had shadowed her ever since.

I am completely and utterly lost. The thought came unbidden and its intensity rattled her weeping anew.

After a while, she lifted her head and looked

around the kitchen. The new KitchenAid mixer her aunt had given them gleamed atop the worn Formica counter. Crystal goblets, still in bubble wrap, lay on their sides waiting to be unwrapped, washed and put away in the painted metal cabinets.

On a table in the corner sat the memory box covered in family photos that Cara had lovingly made and presented to her and Pete at their wedding. One side had been left bare, Cara had tearfully explained, for them to add their own memories.

Sarah smiled through tears at thoughts of her family. She missed them so much. Outside, the rain came down in torrents and somehow, listening to the pattering on the roof made her feel less alone. Rising slowly, she began to clean up the broken plate, one piece at a time.

When she heard the car pull in the drive a while later, she was ready with an apology. *I was feeling lonely and homesick*, she would say. *I just need some time to adjust. Please understand.* She walked to the door to greet him and opened it to find Pete and Cara standing in the doorway, dripping wet.

Sarah's hands flew to her mouth.

Cara smiled. "It was Pete's idea, Sarah. He said you were having a rough time and he flew me here. I would have come last night but they canceled the flights because of the storm. I took the earliest one I could get this morning."

Cara grinned from ear to ear, but Sarah's eyes were on Pete. She wanted to go to him, but shame and embarrassment held her in place.

He nodded at her, just once, and his eyes were warm.

She was forgiven.

Smiling, just slightly, he shrugged off his dripping jacket and closed the door against the rain.

* * *

Remember the Sunrise
by Phyllis Campbell
CWI Contest Finalist 2017

Fall came early on the mountain that year. The leaves turned in mid-September and by the first week in October they lay in sodden heaps under the trees they so recently adorned. They had been so full of life, but now their beauty was gone, and they had no promise for the future.

They're like our lives, Mary thought. She turned the blue Legacy onto the county road that lead to the old farmhouse they had called home ever since Bill came to preach at Meadowview Church. *They have no promise for the future.*

She knew such thoughts were wrong--knew she was questioning God's wisdom in their current problems, but she couldn't help it. She stole a glance at the two people who made up her world.

Bill sat in the passenger seat with sun-bleached hair and brown eyes that would never see again.

Susan, caught in the rearview mirror, smiling her vacant smile.

Mary often wondered what she was thinking. When a child's mind dwelled in a fifteen-year-old body, sometimes even her mother couldn't reach her.

"We can't be sure of the exact cause," Dr. Bradford said the day she was born. "She won't quite be like other children."

Mary remembered how she sobbed against Bill's shoulder as they lay in bed that night. "I am completely and utterly lost," she said. "What did I do wrong? I don't smoke. I don't drink. I don't take drugs. What did I do wrong?"

"Mary, darling, you didn't do anything wrong. It's not your fault, or mine either."

"Bill, what kind of life will she have? We had so many hopes, so many dreams for her."

"She'll have a near normal life, the doctor said. She may not learn as much or as fast, but she'll have a good life."

Mary made a solemn vow to protect her child, no matter what she had to do. It seemed like days later when Susan's second grade teacher wanted to take her class to the zoo.

Mary shook her head. "I'm sorry. No, I can't sign the permission for her to go."

"Do you mind if I ask why?" Miss Herring said.

Mary had said the first thing that came to mind. "The animals will frighten her." The truth was, she didn't want Susan to go anywhere without her.

"But she loves animals," Miss Herring said.

"I know what's best for her!" Mary said, and in

spite of Susan's pleas, she would not change her mind.

The next year, when the teacher made the trip to the Museum of Natural History mandatory, Mary was furious.

"Susan is a special needs student," she said, storming in the principal's office. "You have no right to say she has to take a trip away from her parents."

"Yes, she has special needs," Mrs. Booker replied, "but she does most of her work in the classroom with the other children. This trip is part of a class assignment. We can't force her to go, but it will affect her grade since the students are required to write an essay. Of course, the final decision is yours and your husband's."

"My husband is in full agreement," Mary said, which stretched the truth a bit. Bill's actual words were, "We won't always be here to protect her. We can guide her, but we have to let her find her own way."

"No, Bill! She can't keep up with other children. I can't stand it when they make fun of her. I see the way the kids at church look at her. I can't do much about that, but I *can* pull her out of that school and home school her." But for once, Bill remained firm and Susan remained in school.

Mary mulled over the fifteen years that had passed. She had kept the vow to protect Susan, no matter what. But what would she do now that Bill was blind? He hadn't always agreed with her, but he had always been there, offering strength and love. Now she would have to supply enough love and strength for both.

It all seemed like a bad dream, the kind that suddenly appears after years, taking a different form, but the same old nightmare. Words repeating themselves. "It's normal life; learn to accept it." The words were the same, except the word *blind* had been added and the person most affected was Bill.

Bill called the old gray mare *Patience*. He was fond of saying they'd bought a horse and the old owner threw in a nonworking farm to boot, so Bill rented the fields to the neighboring farmer. There was no practical use for Patience, who plodded along safely, giving leisurely rides to everyone. Leisurely rides until the day Bill rode her and something made her shy. "It was my fault," Bill maintained. "I wasn't expecting her to shy, and off I went."

Now, after three months in extensive rehab therapy, Bill was going home, but not for long. Next week, he would attend the Rehab Center for the Blind, after which he would be able to continue his ministry at the little church where the congregation had been so supportive.

Mary puzzled over these things on the way home. Her main worry wasn't for Bill, although she hated admitting that even to herself. It was for Susan.

How can I possibly give both the care and support they need? Bill accepts and understands he can no longer do the things he's always done, but there's no way Susan will be able to understand the change.

She had been so deep in thought that she almost missed the turn into their driveway. "We're home, everybody," she said forcing her voice to sound cheerful. "Hang on Bill, I'll be around to get you."

"I'll take him," Susan said, hopping out of the car.

"No, Susan." She hadn't meant to speak so sharply, but she conjured up countless accidents with Susan trying to guide her father to the house.

"But, Mom…"

"I'll take care of Daddy. You unlock the door like a good girl."

"I wasn't aware anybody has to *take care of Daddy*," Bill said in a quiet voice.

But Mary, who knew him so well, caught the note of resentment. For that moment, she resented both father and daughter. *I am alone*, she thought, as she fought against tears. *Be strong!*

As she guided Bill to a chair, she was surprised to find Susan frowning at her.

An hour later, a frustrated Mary announced,

"Dinner's ready."

She had eaten with Bill at the rehab center, but this was different. Suppose she did something wrong? They corrected her gently at the center, but here at home she would do what she felt best. They joined hands for grace, and for that brief moment, she felt at peace.

She filled her husband's plate and set it before him. "Bill, your chicken is... uh..." Her mind went blank. How had they told her to describe the location of food on his plate?

"... is at twelve o'clock," Susan finished. "Your peas are at three, broccoli at six, and the roll is at nine."

"Thank you, Susan," Bill said with a smile.

Mary sat staring, amazed. Susan never interrupted adults, and how did she know how to describe the location of food on his plate?

"And your iced tea is... Mom, how do I explain that?"

Mary sat in amazement. "Behind your plate, just a bit to the right," she said.

"Thank you, ladies," Bill said, as he picked up his fork. "You did a good job, Susan. How did you know?"

"There's this girl at school. She's awesome, Daddy. Miss Jarvis, the... Who is she, Mom?"

"The guidance counselor," Mary managed to say.

"Yes. She heard, Daddy, that you would go blind. I'm sorry. I didn't say that right, did I?"

"You're fine, sugar," Bill said. "Go on. She heard I'm blind, and then what?"

"She got me and Cindy together. Oh, yes, I forgot to tell you, Cindy's blind, too. Well, Cindy told me all kinds of good stuff, how to walk with you holding to my arm so you can feel where I'm going, and I wanted to walk in with you, but Mom wouldn't let me."

"I'm sorry," Mary said, supposing she should correct Susan's tone of voice, but she didn't.

"So, Cindy taught you how to identify the location of food on my plate? And what else?" Bill asked.

"All kinds of things. She says you'll learn braille, and how to use a computer with a voice thing that reads the screen. Next year, Cindy's getting a guide dog. Will you get a dog, Daddy?"

"Maybe."

"She helped me fix a card for you, a special kind of card. I'm finished eating. Can I show it to you?"

"But, Susan…" Mary said, pausing. Would her daughter be hurt when she realized he couldn't see the card? Anger boiled to the surface. Anger at the

- 305 -

interfering guidance counselor. Anger with the girl named Cindy. Anger at the whole world, and yes... anger toward God. *I can't take any more!* she thought.

Susan was busy connecting her MP3player to the stereo speakers, her hands shaking with anxiety and excitement. She pushed the button, and the opening notes of Glen Miller's *Sunrise Serenade* filled the room. When the piece finished, Susan's recorded voice came through the speakers.

Remember when Tiger Cat died, Daddy? You showed me the sunrise, and you said God doesn't make bad things happen, but He is always there to give us hope, and He will always be there. You said the sunrise reminds us He is there even though the clouds may cover the sun as it's rising. I love you Daddy.

Tears sprang to Mary's eyes.

Susan wore a puzzled look. "Was it all right?" she said. "I told my friend, Cindy, about the sunrise. She asked what kind of music Daddy likes, and when I told her about the big band stuff, she found this song."

Tears slipped down Mary's cheeks and Bill wiped one eye.

Susan's brow furrowed. "Did I do wrong, because the doctor says he won't see again, Mommy? I'm sorry."

"You did just right, sugar," Bill said, holding

one hand out to Susan and the other to Mary. "I may never see the sun rise again with my physical eyes, but I'll never forget it. That was a beautiful card. Thank you."

Sitting on the porch swing with Mary later that evening, surrounded by the quiet of the night, Bill found her hand and held it. "What's wrong, honey?" he said.

"I've been so wrong for so long," Mary said, sniffing. "I've been so busy trying to protect Susan that I lost sight of the fact that it was God's job. He has given her a very special gift of understanding and love for others, and I failed to see it all these years."

"You know, Mary, she has more faith than both of us put together. There's not a doubt in her mind that I'm going to overcome my blindness."

"Bill, forgive me. I've been doubting it."

"God forgives both of us for doubting, and for forgetting the sunrise that promises His unfailing love. Don't worry. We'll get through this--together."

* * *

The Lucky Ones
by Susan Van Sciver
Judge's Pick

The old ladies meet here at least once a week, usually on Monday. Two come together and within ten minutes the other two join. They kiss each other's cheeks and talk like they've known each other decades. I know they feel like this is "their" diner.

As I wipe the counter, I notice how they put the younger generation to shame with their cleanliness and color-matching, but Barbara wears two much sparkle for my taste. Instead of staring, I divert my eyes to the coffee stain on the counter and scrub it before Big Al gets here. He's a retired cop, and this is his spot. He's a loyal customer, but he always complains about the fancy coffee places and how they charge "nearly five bucks for a cup." Our endless cup of coffee costs under two dollars, but he always leaves a generous tip that probably makes the total as much as the fancy coffee.

I've worked here twelve years, and I liked it better when there were no televisions on the walls stuffing the air with unnecessary information. I take that back--it was a treat at first. I could see what was going on in the world, especially in the area where some of my relatives still live near the desert, and places where US enemies train. I don't look like I come from that part of the world, but that's sheer luck. I'm half Iranian. My hair went gray prematurely, and I favor my mother's Irish side.

Father used to say he was "European, near the Mediterranean." It kept people from asking too many questions. Sometimes he claimed to be Sicilian and spoke with an awful Italian-American accent, dropping the vowels at the end of his words. He really liked those Godfather movies.

"Morning," I say to the four ladies as I walk over to their booth.

"Good morning," they say in unison, watching me fill brown mugs of coffee for all. We have up-to-date features like wi-fi and flat screen televisions, but for some reason, the coffee mugs remain unchanged. They are a watered down dingy brown like the ones that filled my kitchen in the seventies.

I pull my slim notepad out and take their orders. The ladies have never introduced themselves to me, but I've overheard them greet one another. That one is Jeanie, then Barbara, Carol and the chubby one is Mary. They are not old enough to be my mother, but they're motherly. You know the type. Engaged in their grandchildren's lives. They probably have special meals for each one. Undoubtedly, they took homemade cookies and brownies to school for their children. Not like my Mother, who shuttled between jobs at the diner and the laundromat. These ladies took their daughters shopping for back-to-school clothes and wedding dresses. And they negotiated the cost of alterations with my mother. Poor Mother. Scabbed fingers and an aching back.

"One egg, sunny side up, and dry toast," Mary says, bringing me back to earth.

"I'll have a western omelet, dry, and substitute fruit for the home fries," Jeanie says.

"I'll just have coffee," Barbara says.

"And I'll have an English muffin, not burnt, and butter on the side, please," Carol says.

"Great. Be out soon," I say, stuffing my notepad into my apron and making my way to a table of young mothers. A little boy is with them, and I pull a pack of crayons out of my pocket.

These three are dressed in black. Strange. Maybe they're going to exercise. They request coffee and juice and ask me to return for their order. I'm happy to walk away, because the brunette is loud, and doesn't adjust her volume for others. She speaks the way my father did when he mocked Al Pacino.

"I'm not big into meat," she says. "I like steak, but no *saw-sage*. I don't like *pru-shoot*. It's like raw, fatty bacon.*"

The booths are shaped like a horseshoe, and I fill the dingy coffee cups.

I pretend to clean the inside of the display case where the desserts rest just so I can overhear what the old ladies are saying. Their conversations center around vacations and milestones and medical ailments today.

"I don't know what Harry and Matilda are thinking, but they should have stayed with one of us. I can't believe they're staying through the hurricane," Carol says, pointing to the television that shows Hurricane Irma barreling through Florida.

"I'm so glad it turned west. Looks like it will spare Boca," Mary says. I know she has a place there, and I find it funny that she talks about it so much. I wonder if she knows *Boca* means *mouth*.

The other television is set to Fox News, which is showing the tribute to 9/11 victims. I forgot today is the anniversary. It doesn't seem like all of that was sixteen years ago, but it also doesn't seem like there was life before it.

The TV screen splits, showing politicians gathering for the tribute and footage of the actual day. On the left is our President and his Slovenian wife, dressed in a black designer suit and veil, while the right side shows gray-dusted office workers stumbling through an apocalyptic scene.

"There's Donald Trump," the child says with excitement. The sound of his name makes me wince. I rip a sheet from my notepad and walk through the swinging doors to hand it to Eduardo, the cook. He doesn't look up, and he rarely smiles, but we're friends, and I know that he'd deliver fried plantains in the middle of the night if I asked him. Plantains seem to calm my nerves as good as a cigarette. Maybe if Donald Trump tasted Eduardo's plantains, he'd reconsider his immigration policy.

When I get back to the dining room, Martika is seating a couple of mousy women about my age. They are all business, holding folders and wearing wool cardigans. By the time our busboy, Jose, serves their water, the table is covered with papers, manila folders and leather-bound Filofaxes. They'll probably order coffee and leave me a two-buck tip.

The bell dings, and I know the old ladies' food is ready. I could carry diner plates in my sleep without dropping them, so I'm not even thinking as I place the yellow and brown covered plates in front of the foursome, but Barbara's bedazzled black shirt nearly blinds me as the sun glints off the sequins.

My daughter was watching the four ladies with me one day and she said Carol was the "Charlotte" of the group. I didn't know what that meant until I watched a cable program about four ladies in New

York City who discuss sex and fashion. Charlotte is the traditional one amidst flashier types, and so is Carol. Her hair reminds me of Benjamin Franklin's, the way it curls away from her face and up a little at the end, highlighting giant pearl earrings. The others have curled or spiked hair that looks like the product of a beauty parlor.

"Sammy! Why do you have to spill everything!" the loud young mother says. Orange juice flows over the table and onto the floor. I shoot a look to Jose, who's already filling another cup with more juice.

A bell rings on the television, and everyone looks up. The bell marks a moment of silence in honor of when the first plane hit. My life is a string of dinging bells, but this one catches me off-guard. I don't know if we're supposed to cease what we're doing and bow our heads or just carry on. All the diners look up for a quick minute, and return to clicking forks against plates and coffee mugs against Formica.

"God bless Angie," Mary whispers, signing herself with the cross. I don't know if Angie was a victim or if she is a widow because of that plane, but the ladies at the table sit quietly for a moment.

I know Eduardo's cousin worked at Windows on the World. I know my second cousin's husband worked at the dry cleaners across the street. I know I was at home, sick with the flu that day. Sixteen fast years later, here I am.

The middle-aged women in cardigans are holding up flyers and photos and talking about how much money their organization can raise with an auction.

"We can have the photo in a Lucite frame in front of a basket," one says.

"Let's use the cellophane stuff to wrap it up," the shorter of the two says as a large picture of Jerry Seinfeld sits between them. I can imagine Seinfeld's reaction to this scene.

I'm wondering what the deal is with silent auctions. Can't rich people write checks without all the hoopla of a big charity, rubber chickens and gala gowns? I'm sure the real Seinfeld would have something wittier to say.

"Hey, Lila," Big Al says as he settles his wide bottom to the vinyl-covered stool. He looks around as though taking a photo of the scene, just in case something goes awry. Old cop reflexes, I guess.

"Good morning," I say, filling his mug.

"I'm not looking at those televisions. Nothing good there," he says, shaking his head.

I know there's a brotherhood of men he no longer knows because of what the television is showing, so I nod in agreement. The only other thing to talk about is the weather, but I don't want to discuss the hurricane. There should be a reprieve from all weather talk in the Northeast, at least between summer and winter.

I lean forward on the counter to alleviate the pain from the corn on my right foot, and the dull ache in my lower back. I hope Big Al doesn't get political today. I'm not ready to hear him rant against the liberal agenda and the damage Obama has done.

"Did I tell you I was at a conference in San Francisco that day?" Al says to me.

"No, you didn't." That day brings bad memories. Tom and I had saved up for a trip to Napa Valley, but he lost his job and then got cancer. He's in remission now, but we're swamped in credit card debt. Big Al is staring at me and I feel obligated to say something.

Sometimes I feel like I am completely and utterly lost, I think, but instead, I say, "Tom goes for his six-month check up today." I smile, gaze at the horseshoe tables and quickly estimate $25 in tips, which isn't bad for less than an hour of work.

"You always smile when you're worried, Lila," Big Al says. "It's been six months already?"

He doesn't wait for an answer. Just pulls out his billfold and lays $20 on the counter between us.

"Today is a good reminder about how lucky I

am," he says, using the counter to push his body to a standing position.

"This is too much, Al."

"Nah, that's probably what I'd pay for a mocha-chino-latte-thingy," he says with a wink.

* * *

Winter Lilacs
by Cindy Fox
Judge's Pick

Charles stands next to his wife's open casket. A spray of autumn flowers rests on top with an entwined ribbon stenciled *Husband* in glittery gold. The decoration unravels him, too fancy alongside the humble, rust-colored mums--the first flowers he bought for her. His tie cuts into his neck as he bows his head in sorrow, but the tightness in his chest strangles him with shame.

He closes his eyes on his blindness and sees a shower of blinking lights burning holes into his eyelids. Hot tears cling to the corners of his eyes. A steady stream of tinged images flicker through his mind, thinking of the special occasions in their sixty-three years of marriage when he had missed seeing her eyes light up from a bouquet of flowers. He was always looking in the wrong direction.

Muffled conversations in the funeral home divert his private thoughts. His sons stand nearby, arms crossed reverently, while his daughters greet friends and neighbors at the door. His grown grandchildren attempt to hush their children as they fidget on benches that flank the sides of the room.

Menfolk approach him with curt nods and handshakes, their wives standing behind, afraid to touch a man whose wife has died, as if it were contagious.

So sorry, Charles. Yah, that's too bad. Yah. Yah.

Words of condolence are brief. Finnish farmers are too uncomfortable to talk about the death of their neighbor's wife. Better to talk about grain yields, plummeting milk prices, and winter forecast predictions. Charles acknowledges their kindness with nods and welcomes farm talk, a slight reprieve from the day that looms before him.

While the minister prepares for the wake memorial service, mourners fill the seats. Chatter hushes to whispers. A baby cries, then coos as his granddaughter rocks his great grandson at the back of the room.

The minister rubs his shoulder, and says, "It's time."

He turns to face his dear Mary for the last time, her creased forehead and sunken cheeks testaments of hardship and worry. For the first time, her hands are idle, empty. He wishes lilacs were in season. He'd tuck a cluster of their tiny cross-like blossoms between her folded hands, but fall chills the air. It's a time for dying. He turns away from her pinched lips sagging in an eternal frown and walks with the hunched, painful gait of a man whose shoes are too small for his feet.

Though the pew is only steps away, the distance stretches long and empty.

Later, back at the farmhouse, her absence is so palpable it is almost a presence. A bib apron hangs lifelessly on a peg by the wood stove. The stove is cold, the coffee pot empty. In the bedroom, his weathered hands clumsily loosen his tie. Sitting on the bed, he unlaces his shoes as his eyes linger on her hairbrush, a small glass bowl of bobby pins, and her Finnish Bible laying on the vanity.

His forlorn image in the mirror, a face etched with deep crevices and fissures, cracks. He buries his face in his trembling hands. Normally, a man who does not show emotion, now wails like an old church organ in the quiet of the farmhouse. Then he lays awake on her side of the bed wondering how he can go on without her. To the ceiling's blank space, he mutters, "I am completely and utterly alone."

In days to come, well-meaning relatives and neighbors come to console and offer their support in the form of Finnish food--homemade meat and potato pies, flatbread, and spicy apple cakes. He thanks them for their goodwill, but is reluctant to engage in further conversation. Visitors stand around the door and the kitchen table, but unconsciously back themselves out the door to let him grieve alone.

For the better part of two years, grief comes and

goes like the seasons, most painful during long Minnesota winters when he is confined to the house. Pinpricks of guilt needle him for not being a better husband, but over time, remorse heals into a scar. Loneliness continues to fester like an open wound. Alone. Yet never alone.

One early evening in late December, her shadows follow him around the house. He grumbles to himself in Finn, half-expecting to hear her feisty retort, but the only sound is the tick-tock of the clock, counting his time on earth in slow, deliberate increments. He misses their petty arguments. If she were here, she'd scold him for not changing his overalls, caked to a greasy sheen after puttering away the daylight hours.

Fingers laced over a crossed knee, his thumbs caress the denim patch where her fingers mended the ragged hole. He remembers the Singer's needle crunching deep on the first stitch. He bobs his head, coaxing the image forward. As her feet pumped the treadle, the sewing machine had chugged like a slow-moving train, and the belt whistled along with the rocking rhythm. At each corner, her nimble fingers lifted the needle foot, swiveled the pant leg around, and she and the machine hummed until their work was done. After clipping the threads, she held up his overalls and they looked like new. No, he now reflects, they looked better than brand-new.

He recalls when she'd made bib aprons from faded kitchen curtains. Curtains she claimed were too good to drag dirt across the floor in the form of a rag mop, while store-bought aprons, practical gifts from their daughters, remain tucked in her cedar chest. Still in their original packaging. Unopened. Never worn.

She liked sewing in the morning. It was cool in the summer and gave the best light in winter. The Singer still sits in the kitchen next to the east window, clinging to grime that waits for her dust rag. He stares out the window, now hazy without her sparkling touch, and he thinks the house misses her, too.

Between the gravel road and their house, she'd insisted he plant a row of lilac bushes. At the time, he thought her wish was to keep the dust away from the house, but now he recollects her standing by the lilacs breathing in their heady perfume. With a bouquet in each hand, she'd brought them into the house and set them in jelly jars on the kitchen table. The aroma of lilacs was pleasing he had to admit, but more so, because the scent had pleased her. He promises himself to bring lilacs in next spring.

Charles shivers to shake off the chill creeping into the house. He slowly rises to loosen winter's icy fingers that grip his aching bones, shuffles across the room, scuffing leather slippers across the worn linoleum floor. He shoves more wood into the stove, and the flames lick at the dry oak. The fire crackles a distant reminder when she'd cooked on the wood-burning stove, stirring a pot of Finnish *mojakka*, a hearty soup made from yesterday's leftovers. He swallows an ache in his throat when he thinks how she prepared appetizing meals out of nothing.

His own cooking tastes bland, always lacking a pinch of some secret ingredient. He opens the refrigerator door, steps back from the odor of spoiled food, and suddenly isn't hungry anymore. Dirty dishes in the sink and the splattered countertop nag at him as if she is looking over his shoulder, but he's too tired.

He is tired, too, of being angry at her for moving ahead without him. He looks up at the ceiling and knows she'd shake her head at him for going to bed mad, but it wouldn't be the first time. They were stubborn Finns. One time they'd banged heads so hard they hadn't spoken to each other for a week. But he admired her *sisu*, the lively spunk that was now a silent void in the long days.

Later in the evening, he closes his eyes to her shadows and finds solace that only sleep can bring. He lies on the bed they'd shared for over sixty years, missing her warmth and the wood smoke smell of her hair and skin. He rolls into the slight hollow where her petite body used to rest and folds his hands to pray.

He thanks God for blessing his life. He has seen His creative power in the faces of his newborn children and grandchildren, tasted His bounty in fields of ripened wheat and golden ears of corn, and heard the welcome thunder and splash of raindrops on a drought-ridden year. Though he is grateful for all the things that he and Mary shared over the years, he asks Him for one last request.

He feels His presence when a sharp pain crushes his chest. Hugging her pillow close to his heart, the pain slowly subsides, and calmness covers him like a warm blanket. As his eyes close for the last time, he senses the sweetness of lilacs filling the bedroom, because eternity cannot douse the drifting scent of love.

* * *

~*~

If you enjoyed ***Lost! A themed anthology 2017***, please consider leaving a review on Amazon.

~*~

Short story contest entries were judged on originality, creativity, style and technique.

A great story can score well in the first two categories but lose marks if grammar, punctuation and spelling are incorrect and if paragraphs are poorly formatted.

Learn how to write professionally at Creative Writing Institute, where every student receives a private tutor. It could be the difference between a top placement, being a finalist, or missing a top spot.

With permission, the contest stories have been edited for this publication while trying to maintain the intent of the original entry.

You can find our previous anthologies on Amazon -

Explain: A themed anthology 2016
Bargain: A themed anthology 2015
Wrong: A themed anthology 2014
Overruled: A themed anthology 2013

Acknowledgements

Welcome to Creative Writing Institute's fifth anthology! This collection contains short stories written by the 2017 Short Story Contest winners, runners-up, other stories selected for the anthology, stories written by invited guests, contest judges, Creative Writing Institute Staff, and best-selling authors, Mikel Wilson and Robin Currie.

We would especially like to thank Southern Star Publishing and editor, Jay Hirst, for making our fifth anthology a reality. No one knows or realizes the effort Jay puts into this service, and never charges a penny for it. Words fail me except to say God bless you richly for your kindness to me and to Creative Writing Institute.

We also extend our gratitude to proof readers Jianna Higgins, Krysti Miller, Jennifer Doss and Janet Lopes. This is a long and tiring job.

Thank you, Jianna Higgins, for acting as head judge this year and to the following tutors who helped judge the short story entries:

    Coordinating judge: S. Joan Popek
    Judge: L. Edward Carroll
    Judge: Emily-Jane Hills Orford
    Judge: Kim Cawley

Thank you so much to literary agent, Cyle Young of Hartline Agency, for writing our Foreword.

And that brings us to those who have so kindly allowed us to publish their work in our 2017 anthology. We are behind you, supporting you, rooting for you, and yes, even *pushing* a little as you march forth into the writing world.

Last, but not least, we thank you, the reader, for supporting these authors and Creative Writing Institute by ordering your copy of CWI's 2017 anthology. Without you, all efforts would be in vain.

Creative Writing Institute

Creative Writing Institute is an online writing school that provides a variety of writing courses and a private tutor for every student. Our classes are open year round, which means you can begin your course right now. If you need financial assistance, we offer a no interest payment plan.

CWI is a charity that sponsors cancer patients in free writing courses. In addition, we have constructed our courses so visually impaired students can use adaptive devices to enlarge or convert text into electronically synthesized speech.

Our goal:
- We will evaluate you quickly and personally escort you to your highest potential. We will encourage your heart and sharpen your mind.

Our pledge:
- We will tailor your class to meet your needs, aptitude and desires.
- You will have a private tutor who will provide quick and professional assistance all the way through your course.
- You will never be a number to us. Your tutor will interact with you all the way through your course.

Please… <u>believe in yourself</u>. Invest in yourself.

If you will make writing a priority, we will do everything within our power to make your writing dreams come true. Start climbing that ladder to the stars today!

Courses:
- Punctuation Review
- Back to Basics Grammar Review
- Dynamic Nonfiction
- Creative Writing 101
- Short Story Safari
- Novel Writing Made Easy
- Writing your Memoirs
- Writing for Children
- Writing for the Middle Grades
- Writing for the Young Adult
- Fantasy in Flight
- Horror House
- Flashing your Fiction
- Fundamentals of Poetry
- Advanced Wordsmithing - coming soon
- Famous Women Poets - coming soon

All classes are suitable for visually impaired students

Payment plans available at no interest.

Contact **DeborahOwen@CWinst.com**
http://www.CreativeWritingInstitute.com/

Made in the USA
San Bernardino, CA
04 December 2017